"PLEASE," HE SAID SOFTLY,
"DON'T BE ALARMED."

She looked at him intently and smiled. "You shouldn't be up here. You're spoiling—"

"Listen to me. I'm going to reach my hand out to you and help you off that ledge."

"No, I'm sorry, but this is something I have to do," she said with determination.

"No, it isn't. I'll make a deal with you. Come inside and we'll talk. If I can't convince you, there are other alternatives. . . ."

"It's kind of nice to know someone could care so much about a perfect stranger. I mean, here you are, wanting to rescue me. What's your name?" she asked abruptly.

"Luke—Dr. Lucas Eliot."

"Luke," she said with a sweet smile. "I have to jump. Honest."

CANDLELIGHT ECSTASY SUPREMES

TAMED SPIRIT

Alison Tyler

A CANDLELIGHT ECSTASY SUPREME

Published by
Dell Publishing Co., Inc.
1 Dag Hammarskjold Plaza
New York, New York 10017

Dell ® TM 681510, Dell Publishing Co., Inc.

Candlelight Ecstasy Supreme is a trademark of
Dell Publishing Co., Inc.

Candlelight Ecstasy Romance®, 1,203,540, is a registered
trademark of Dell Publishing Co., Inc.

ISBN: 0-440-18508-4

Printed in the United States of America

First printing—December 1984

To Our Readers:

Candlelight Ecstasy is delighted to announce the start of a brand-new series—Ecstasy Supremes! Now you can enjoy a romance series unlike all the others—longer and more exciting, filled with more passion, adventure, and intrigue—the stories you've been waiting for.

In months to come we look forward to presenting books by many of your favorite authors and the very finest work from new authors of romantic fiction as well. As always, we are striving to present the unique, absorbing love stories that you enjoy most—the very best love has to offer.

Breathtaking and unforgettable, Ecstasy Supremes will follow in the great romantic tradition you've come to expect *only* from Candlelight Ecstasy.

Your suggestions and comments are always welcome. Please let us hear from you.

Sincerely,

The Editors
Candlelight Romances
1 Dag Hammarskjold Plaza
New York, New York 10017

CHAPTER ONE

There was an eerie sense of quiet as Luke Eliot slid his gray Triumph into the garage, but he was too sick to notice. Anyway, how often was he around the neighborhood at eleven in the morning?

He sneezed loudly just as he pulled up the emergency brake. In the dimly lit garage he rifled through his jacket pocket for a tissue as he sneezed again. Pressing the back of his hand against his forehead, his skin felt hot to the touch. With his other hand he pushed the elevator button impatiently and quickly got inside.

If he hadn't scheduled two patients that morning, he probably wouldn't have gotten out of bed in the first place—or at least not at six-thirty in the morning.

Mrs. Diamond could have survived without her session; she'd spent her whole fifty minutes describing in excruciating detail the cocktail party she had given the night before. Last week she had used their hour to agonize over the planning of that same party. Maybe next week, if he was lucky, they could replay the event one more time. Hours like the ones with Connie Diamond sometimes made Luke Eliot wonder why he had chosen psychiatry as his area of medicine. Then he remembered forty-three-year-old Howie Jordan, his other patient that morning. Howie was struggling with anxiety that kept him tied to his mother and a job he hated. Today, after months of meeting together, Howie had said he'd actually put down a deposit on his own apartment. It was a big victory, and Luke's miserable flu notwithstanding, he had felt that exhilarating sense of elation that came from having helped someone.

When he got to his door, Luke fumbled for his key. Letting himself inside, he quickly removed his wet raincoat, hanging it carefully on the standing brass coatrack in the hall. San Francisco had been going through a record-breaking month of rain. It was letting up as he left his office, but it was still bleak. The gloomy weather perfectly matched Luke's mood as he stretched out wearily on the couch, hanging his feet over the edge. Closing his eyes, he tried to comfort himself by contemplating his upcoming trip to Greece. In less than three weeks he would be lying on a lushly hot Aegean beach, his eyes cast up at a brilliant blue sky, his mind concentrating only on the sound of sea and surf. . . . Ah, Greece.

Two months on that ancient isle and he would come back to San Francisco revitalized. And hopefully with a completed manuscript. He would give himself one full week to unwind, to do nothing but loll around on the beach and take in the sights, and then he would spend the next seven weeks scrupulously adhering to a self-enforced schedule of writing mornings and evenings, with afternoons off—for good behavior. He smiled to himself. The plan suited him nicely. Luke Eliot always worked best under a carefully structured routine.

A cold shiver reminded him that he ought to take some aspirin. He was a man who hated being sick. Even today, as awful as he felt, the only way he could give himself permission to go home was to promise himself that after a brief rest he would continue working on his book. Right now, the thought of lifting up a pencil made him wince. He forced himself to get up and find the aspirin.

Sliding open the medicine cabinet, he found an old plastic cup with a solitary toothbrush inside, a couple of throwaway razors, a large bottle of mouthwash, and a couple of vials of pills prescribed by Dr. Teri Caulfield. Teri was a top-notch internist as well as Luke's occasional girl friend. She had treated him for a strep throat infection over a year ago and since then, a pleasant if not overly passionate relationship had developed. Both of them were busy with their practices and all the extracurricular activities that accompanied their work, leaving little time for a very active social life. Luke found their casual involvement perfectly satisfactory, since his plans for the next couple of years didn't include any close personal relationships. For a moment he considered calling Teri about his flu but decided he could do without her likely diatribe about how poorly he took care of himself.

A couple of aspirins would do the trick, he decided. Only there weren't any in the bathroom. He vaguely remembered seeing some in one of the kitchen cabinets. A cold breeze hit him as he stepped into the kitchen. And then he remembered why. His coordination had been disastrous that morning. He'd spilled the instant coffee, knocked over the sugar bowl, and completed the fiasco by burning the toast. Not your ordinary black, charred bread. For some reason the stuff actually burst into flames. God only knows what chemical additives they mixed that loaf up with. He had opened the window to air out the kitchen, and typical of how his day was going, he'd forgotten to close it.

A good-size puddle was slowly becoming a meandering stream underneath the window on the quarry tile floor. Shivering, he threw a large wad of paper toweling on the floor and hurried over to close the window.

That was when he saw her. He stood at his kitchen window staring in transfixed amazement. And then he whispered, "Oh, my God!"

She was across the road, in the new high-rise apartment house that had only just been completed. Well, not exactly in the house. To be precise, she was standing on the window ledge of the fourth floor, in a direct line from Luke's own apartment. A slender, solitary figure poised on a thin concrete slab a good fifty feet above the ground, the wind whipping angrily around her.

A hallucination, he thought immediately, shaking his head for clarity. She hadn't budged. He gasped, convinced of the reality, of the inevitability of the woman's fateful end. At the very moment Luke took it all in, he raised his hand up in a frantic stop, wait-for-me motion. His head was spinning. If she didn't get off that ledge pretty soon and back inside, she was going to die of pneumonia instead of a fall.

He couldn't have stood at that window for more than a few seconds. Already a crowd was gathering below, the area cordoned off. Obviously, someone already had called the police. There were several squad cars, and the area was lit up. Luke saw a couple of cameras and realized that newsmen were usually only a few steps behind the cops when there was any hint of a story. He knew he had to get to the woman before she did something crazy.

He forgot about the window, the puddle, and his cold as he barreled out of his apartment, leaving his damp raincoat hanging on the coatrack.

He flew down the stairs, never considering the elevator. "Wait for me," he whispered frantically. "Wait for me, lady."

Breathlessly, he raced across the street. The crowd was growing by the minute. Suicide attempts clearly attracted a lot of interest. Luke looked up. She was still there. He shoved against people, elbowing them out of his way. Making his way to the other side of the street, he spotted a cop at the front entrance. He ducked into the alleyway leading to the back door. It was propped open but there was no one in sight. Luke slipped inside before a policeman reappeared and tried to stop him. This wasn't the time for explanations and examination of credentials. Time, Luke knew, was crucial. Any moment might be too late. He paused at the bottom flight of stairs just long enough to catch his breath. Panting, he somehow propelled himself upward, taking the stairs two and three steps at a time.

It wasn't too difficult to calculate which apartment was hers. Only three of them faced east to the street, and Luke had noted that her window was a center one. Until he reached for the handle, the thought of the door being locked hadn't entered his mind. He was reasonably strong and in good shape for thirty-six, but he'd never had to test his strength by knocking down a door. Fortunately, this one was unlocked.

Quietly, so as not to alarm her, Luke crossed the living room. That was odd. The room was empty. Not even a rug on the floor. Every psychiatrist has to be part detective, uncovering information that at varying times patients either won't or are unable to share. Now Luke put the empty room together with the woman's actions and began to form a hypothesis. This was a lady who had seen good times—possibly some wealthy old guy's mistress—who was suddenly having the rug pulled out from under her. How literal could he get? he wondered, as he crossed the hardwood floor, his leather loafers squishing with each step. He caught a sneeze before it erupted. Now that would be fitting irony. He races out of his sickbed to save a woman from suicide and scares her right off the ledge with an explosive sneeze. Terrific.

He edged near the window now, giving himself a chance to observe her before she realized he was there. She was young, maybe in her mid-twenties, and she was wearing an expensive-looking evening gown that was soaking wet. Whatever her problem, she had obviously been walking in the rain that morning, possibly trying to sort out what to do. Luke figured she hadn't bothered changing from her night out—a night that had caused enough pain to lead to her standing on that ledge. Luke also noticed something else. The woman was gorgeous. Even with her thick black hair plastered down around her face, she was something. He had read about women with coal-black eyes the size of saucers. This was the *real* thing. And skin—porcelain white around the outline of her full breasts above the low-cut gown, the rest of her tanned a warm, golden bronze. A Greek goddess, Luke thought, distracted for a split second by the vision.

And then she spotted him. Out of the corner of her eye, she saw him in shadow.

"Please," he said softly, "don't be alarmed." He could see the shock registering on her face. It was important to remain calm. Above all else, don't let her panic. He was still out of breath, but he tried to keep his voice controlled.

"I just want to talk to you. I'm a doctor. I'd like to help."

She shifted slightly. Luke hurried on. "As terrible as things may seem to you at this moment, almost nothing is ever really that bad."

She looked at him more intently, almost analytically. "How did you get up here?"

"Why I—I saw you. I want to help. Look, why don't you come inside and we'll talk about it? You'd be amazed how helpful it can be to talk things out with someone who can be objective and yet sympathetic. Come inside. It's really miserable out there."

She still looked a bit puzzled, but then she smiled. She actually smiled.

Okay, good, he thought. She still has a sense of humor—maybe even a sense of the absurd. She didn't seem too edgy, either. Another good sign. And she seemed willing to listen to him. Luke was beginning to feel more confident.

"You shouldn't be here," she whispered. "You're spoiling—"

"Listen to me for a minute. Whatever reason you've got for thinking this is the only solution, is wrong. It's something you decided in a moment of desperation. And that's the worst time to make a decision."

"You don't understand," she whispered again, her agitation seeming to mount.

He was getting nowhere. He had to get her

inside. Sounding as authoritative and demanding as he could, he said, "I'm going to reach my hand out to you and help you inside."

She took a wide step away from the window. "I can't. I'm sorry. This is something I have to do," she said with determination, no longer bothering to whisper.

She had a deep voice—throaty and very sexy. What a thing to think about at a time like this! he chided himself.

"No, it isn't. I'll make a deal with you. Come inside and we'll talk about it. Then if I can't convince you there are other alternatives . . ."

She turned her head to him, her large black eyes blinking rapidly. "It's kind of nice to know someone could care so much about a perfect stranger. I mean, here you are, knowing nothing at all about me, wanting to rescue me. It's really very comforting." She gave him a dazzling smile.

And then it hit him. Of course, that was it. This gorgeous creature with her lovely eyes and beautiful smile was nuts, bonkers, insane. He was going to have to humor her.

"I may not know much about you, but I don't feel as though you're a stranger. In fact, I have an intuitive sense that I do know you a little," he said in his soothingly professional voice. "Besides"—he smiled warmly—"it isn't a good day for jumping. It's cold and damp and you're all wet."

She giggled and then burst out laughing. Luke got more nervous. It wouldn't do to have her fall

17

off the ledge due to a fit of hysterics at his ludi-
crous remark. Maybe she wasn't crazy after all.

He tried another way. "What's your name?"

She was still too far down the ledge for him to
reach her, but she hadn't taken her eyes off him.
Her gaze was mysterious; the original anxiety and
shock seemed to have given way to curiosity,
interest, and something else—something Luke
couldn't define. Under other circumstances he might
have read humor into those coal-colored eyes, as if
there were a part of her that was actually enjoying
herself thoroughly. Maybe it was the attention.
But Luke found it hard to believe this ravishing
beauty did not often get that. No, it must be
something else.

"I'm Catherine Roy," she introduced herself
politely. They might have been sipping drinks at a
cocktail party. "My friends all call me Cat."

"Cat." He nodded. He would show her he meant
to be her friend as well. "Cat," he repeated, "you
are a beautiful young woman. Really, you are. And
I'm sure you have a great deal to offer. . . ."

What was he saying? And why was she smiling
more broadly?

"You are very attractive yourself, doctor," she
responded, her voice even throatier, a definite
sparkle in those big black eyes.

She was actually flirting with him. What kind of
a woman flirts with a perfect stranger while she's
perched on a ledge in the pouring rain contemplating suicide?

"That sounds like a bad cold," she went on as he

18

tried to drown a cough. "If I wasn't—uhm, busy—I could make up a batch of my special cold remedy for you. It's an old family secret."

He latched on to her remark. "That's a shame. A real shame. I've tried everything for this flu and nothing works. I do feel rotten. What if—what if you came inside and whipped up some of that secret recipe and then if—if you still want to go back out there you can." Once he got her inside he'd be able to get her to the hospital, and she'd get the help she needed.

"You'd better go back to bed before you get any sicker." Her voice held real concern.

"What about you?"

"Don't worry about me. I'll be okay in just a little while." She leaned forward slightly as she spoke. "It was really nice talking to you," she added, a cool note of finality in her voice.

"Cat. Don't jump. Please. I've just gotten to know you. I'd like to get to know you better. I'd like to help you." He meant it. Something had gone haywire for her, but if she could get whatever it was straightened out, he really did want to—to what? He wasn't sure. All he knew was that Cat Roy was a strikingly beautiful woman who, even under these insane circumstances, had an intense appeal.

"What's your name?" she asked abruptly.

"Luke—Dr. Lucas Eliot."

"Luke," she said with a sweet smile that pierced his heart. "I have to jump. Honest."

He saw the look in her eye. She meant it.

19

"Cat!" he screamed as she let go, her body falling weightless, her black hair flying in the wind. Luke fell against the wall, stunned, aghast. No, no, no, was all he could think. He couldn't hear the impact, but his imagination was gruesome enough. And then, swallowing hard, certain he was about to be sick, he forced himself to move to the window and look down for the first time.

"What the—" Within a flash, the expression on his face switched drastically. He was speechless, frozen to the spot, unable to believe the scene below.

Cat Roy had made a perfect landing—not onto the cold, hard concrete pavement below but into a huge inflated mattress. Now she was casually being helped off by some guy in a rain slicker who handed her a thick towel and coat. She looked up as she slipped on the raincoat and met Luke's stunned stare.

"Thanks, Doc." She waved. "Told you I'd be okay." She started off and then turned back to him. "If things ever do get that bad for me, Doc, I sure hope somebody like you will be around."

A man who was standing off to the side near the cameraman who, in Luke's frantic rush across the street he had mistaken for a newsman, came out from his shelter.

"Hey you, buddy."

Luke stared openmouthed down at the man.

"That was a great improvisation. I'd like to use it in the film. There's a nice little paycheck in it for you. What do you say?"

Luke did not say a word. Instead he slammed the window shut, stormed out of the empty apartment, and, not bothering to wait for the elevator this time, either, flew down the stairs two at a time.

His harangue would have been a lot more effective if he could have stopped coughing, sneezing, and losing his voice. However, he did manage to make his point to the director, who silently nodded at him with a look of disappointment and bewilderment on his face. Most people would give their eyeteeth to be in a major motion picture.

As for Cat Roy, Luke did not waste any words. One long glower got his point across. She gave him another of those earth-moving smiles, but this time Luke was angry enough to be immune. He stormed off across the street to his apartment, ignoring the large puddles he stepped in along the way.

CHAPTER TWO

His temperature read 102 degrees, but Luke was convinced the thermometer wasn't registering properly. He'd been doing a slow boil for the last two hours, and he knew his temperature had to be skyrocketing. He pulled his flannel robe more tightly around his chilled frame and tossed the thermometer on the coffee table. He leaned back on the couch, waiting for pneumonia to overtake him. There couldn't be a more fitting end to this insane day.

When Luke first got back to his apartment, he stalked the rooms with a fury, practically tearing off his drenched shoes and trousers, tossing them mindlessly around the apartment. Finally, when he'd stood under a hot shower long enough for his teeth to stop chattering, the anger began to subside, leaving in its place an even worse feeling of utter foolishness. The whole scene—his bursting in on the filming of a movie, trying to rescue some damn actress playing a part of a suicidal maniac, being asked permission to use his inadvertent role—made him feel sicker than the rotten flu did.

His anger resurfaced. That woman had not only made a fool out of him, but she'd also had a grand time doing it. While he'd stood there, his shoes wet, chilled to the bone, beseeching her not to kill herself, she had herself a good old chuckle watching him make an ass out of himself. No wonder there were fewer and fewer do-gooders in this world. He risks his failing health to try to save her life, and she leads him on right to the finish. Boy, would he like to get his hands on her, he fumed. His anger triggered off a sneezing fit. In the middle of it the doorbell rang.

He opened the door on the last sneeze.

Cat Roy, dried off and wearing the very latest in Western fashion, from the chocolate-brown suede Stetson hat to the studded riding boots, a fringed white leather jacket and tight-fitting jeans in between, leaned against the door jamb.

"How did you get into the building? You didn't buzz." His voice cracked, partly from the cold and partly from shock.

"Some nice young guy who lives here held the lobby door open for me. He even helped me locate your apartment number on the mailbox. I guess he didn't think I looked too dangerous."

Luke could have argued the point, but he was too busy coughing.

"Your cold sounds worse," she said in that throaty voice Luke had already become familiar with.

"I wonder why," Luke said sarcastically. "Have you come to wheedle my consent to use that piece of film, or did you simply need another laugh?"

She grinned, removing her cowboy hat, her thick mane cascading down around her shoulders. Luke, as angry as he was, did not fail to notice that with her hair no longer dripping wet around her face, she was even more ravishing than she had been when he saw her out on that ledge.

"It was a great dramatic moment," she said with a crooked little smile, which, on her face, looked sexy. "But Carl decided it wasn't right, after all. We'll have to shoot it over again."

"How disappointing," he mocked. "You'll have to forgive me if I beg out on the retake. Hollywood will have to wait."

"You were good," Cat offered.

"And that for a guy who didn't even get a chance to memorize the right lines." He gave her a searing stare. "This should teach me not to make house calls."

"I'm sorry."

Luke studied her more closely as she looked contritely at him. She stepped closer. He turned away.

"Forget it," he grumbled.

"No, honestly. I shouldn't have misled you like—"

"Misled me," he roared, sweeping around to gape at her with disbelief, his hands thrown up in

24

a gesture of amazement. "That's beautiful. That's the best understatement I've heard all year. Do you realize, young woman, that you might have—have given me a coronary. Sorry, you tell me. Sorry . . . ." He fired the words at her, his hands still poised in midair.

Cat met Luke's eyes directly. She'd wondered about their color this morning, but the water running from her hair into her eyes had not allowed a careful inspection. They were green, she saw now—a warm, misty heather. Even in his rage, his eyes maintained that soft hue. And a striking look of sincerity.

She liked the way he looked—lean, crisp, sharp, without the pretty-boy features she had become all too familiar with over the years, growing up with actors and stunt men on Hollywood back lots. With Luke there were no affected glances or studied poses, no macho-cool mannerisms or trendy come-ons. Dr. Luke Eliot was a new and different breed. He was straightforward and refreshingly honest, even if his candor was a trifle painful at this particular moment. Cat shifted her cowboy hat from one hand to the other.

"I guess you're still mad," she said, making some attempt to look repentant. It didn't quite come off. "Could you finish scolding me inside? I've had a hectic day and I'm wiped out." Her eyes shone with humor despite Luke's harangue. "Besides, I brought you a peace offering." She extended a Thermos bottle. "My secret cold remedy. From the look of it, Doctor, you could use some."

"How thoughtful, Miss Roy. And here I was going on about how little you cared for my welfare." He gave her a facetious grimace. Without having made a conscious decision, he found that he had stepped aside, allowing Cat access to the apartment.

As she walked in she said, "I was pretty confident I wouldn't cause a coronary." She let her glance deliberately scan over his body. Luke felt oddly uncomfortable standing there clad in his well-worn bathrobe for her inspection. Refusing to be intimidated—after all, in his profession, he had learned that lesson well—he fixed her with a cool and hopefully intimidating glare. It had little effect on Cat.

"You look too vigorous for premature heart failure," Cat commented lightly. "Except for that cold, Doctor, I'd say you were quite fit. This little drink of mine should soon fix what's ailing you."

"A homespun physician as well as an actress. Quite a lot of accomplishments for one lady."

"I'm not an actress," Cat corrected.

"Of course. When you jumped off that ledge, a movie crew just happened by and not only caught you, but also signed you up for a part. Not as tame as Schwab's Drugstore for a discovery but quite creative. Or was it just your lucky day?"

Cat sat on the edge of an armchair, hand cupping her chin. "You're cute when you're angry."

"I am never cute," he balked.

Cat laughed. Luke glowered for a moment and then laughed, too.

"I'm a stunt woman," Cat said as she took in the neat, well-organized living room, save for a pair of slacks haphazardly crumpled against a tidy magazine rack. "Liz Fuller is the star of the film. I take all of her falls, collisions, and an assortment of other dangers." She walked over to the sofa, leaned against the arm, then casually slid back, landing on the cushion, her long, slender legs draped over the side. "God, I'm exhausted."

She yawned, stretching. As she unbuttoned her jacket, revealing a form-fitting cowboy shirt, Luke fought to repress a flash of arousal. He was still angry at her, didn't know her from Adam, and as much as she provoked his fantasies, he never did like women who called the shots. If Cat Roy was providing herself as well as her no-doubt-drugged medicinal drinks as a peace offering, he was not biting. At least not yet.

"Look, Miss Roy. I've had a rather harrowing day myself," he said curtly. "I'm sick, I have some work to do, and I have a seven A.M. patient tomorrow morning. So," he said, bending over her, grabbing her elbow and helping her up, "if you don't mind, the fun and games are over. You've had your laugh. Maybe someday down the line I might have a chuckle over the whole ridiculous scene myself, but right now I am not in a pleasant mood. Do you get my drift, Miss Roy?"

"It was Cat when you thought I was about to die. If I remember correctly, you told me you would like to get to know me better." She tugged away from his grasp. "And you begged me to whip up some of my cold remedy for you. So I did." She sighed. "Where's the kitchen?"

"What?"

"I have to heat this stuff up, and then you can drink it down. I guarantee you'll feel a lot better very soon."

"Please—please go home. I don't want your— your brew. I'm not into drugs. Good old orange juice, aspirin, and as much sleep as possible are the only remedies for the flu. I'm a doctor, I should know."

Cat was already on her way to the kitchen. She had no trouble finding it, since there were only three rooms in the apartment.

He followed her in, still protesting. "Are you always like this? You walk into a total stranger's apartment and simply take over?"

"You're not a total stranger," she muttered, her head inside a cabinet as she rummaged for a pot. "You saved my life. Or you would have, if it had needed saving. I owe you."

Luke took hold of her wrist as she carried the pot to the stove. "Do me a favor. Don't owe me, okay? Just go away. I'm going to pretend this whole day was nothing but a bad dream. I'll make believe you were simply a gorgeous figment of my imagination."

"Thanks for the compliment, Doctor. I was beginning to think you might not like girls." She grinned impishly.

Luke sputtered for a moment, then, seeing her laughing eyes, sighed. "I give up." He took a deep breath. "What's in that concoction, anyway?" he asked warily.

"Don't worry. I'm a vegetarian and I don't believe in drugs. There's nothing in here but a marvelous blend of herbs, roots, and seaweed," she said enthusiastically.

"Not only don't I believe in all that healing mumbo jumbo, but even if I did, there is no way I would drink that—that . . ."

"Nonsense," she scolded softly. "It happens to taste great. Don't think about the ingredients if they don't appeal to you." She tested the brew with her pinky finger, slipping her finger into her mouth afterward. "Perfect."

Luke found her gesture surprisingly erotic. For a second he forgot about the drink altogether. Until she poured it into a mug and offered it to him.

"Really Cat, I—I can't drink that. I—I'm feeling better, anyway. Yes, really, this flu is probably breaking." He pressed his palm against his head for emphasis. "No more fever."

Cat stepped closer. She took his hand away, replacing it with her own cool palm. Shaking her head, she murmured, "You're losing your touch, Doctor. Your head is hotter than burning embers. Here," she insisted, pushing the drink into his hand.

Luke noticed that her eyes weren't really black—more a midnight blue. Maybe they changed with the weather—or her mood. He was still thinking about her eyes as well as how good her touch felt when he took the first sip, Cat standing close to him, those dark, intriguing eyes of hers watching him carefully.

He took a second taste. "Well, it's not as awful as I thought it would be." Then he added, "You sure you didn't slip anything illegal into this?"

"Drink up. Doctor's orders." Cat smiled. Once she was convinced he would finish it, Cat walked back into the living room. He followed her in and found her standing at his desk, idly scanning the surface, her eyes coming to rest on one large pile of papers.

Luke nervously moved toward the desk, blocking her view.

"You do a lot of writing for a doctor," she observed blithely. "What kind of physician are you, anyway?"

"I'm a psychiatrist," he answered, more officiously than he meant. What was she smiling about now?

"Oh," was all she said as she continued to focus on the desk, despite Luke's attempt to play interference. "What are you writing? Everyone's deep, dark secrets?"

Luke folded his arms across his chest. Again sounding officious, he said, "What happens between a psychiatrist and his patient is strictly confidential. . . ."

"I'm teasing," Cat said, patting his shoulder as though he were a small child. "I haven't needed your kind of services myself, but in the business I'm in, plenty of people I know do."

Luke would have enjoyed telling her not to be so sure she didn't need her head examined. What kind of woman makes a career out of jumping out of windows? However, he bit his tongue. He always made a point of abstaining from professional analyses with anyone other than patients.

Instead, he said wryly, "Teasing seems to be something you enjoy doing. How fortunate for you I'm so gullible."

"Oh, I don't think that. You impress me as a shrewd, intelligent, caring kind of guy. Nobody else came running to my rescue today. And you had a good line. I honestly think if I were planning to kill myself, you could have talked me out of it. I bet you're very successful in your work."

"I am, as a matter of fact," he said, the officiousness gone. He smiled. "I'm amazed at your analysis, though. I certainly would not have formed the same conclusions witnessing my ridiculous behavior this afternoon. I still don't know how I mistook those cameras for TV news equipment. I guess I was too worried about you." His glance drifted over her face. "I'm usually a lot more observant."

"I did try to explain." She grinned. "But you were so determined to save me, I didn't get the chance to finish. Then, well . . . Once Carl spotted you at the window, he pulled back behind the car and motioned me to—to play out the new scene. He's like that, believes in letting his cast try new ideas, improvise."

31

"Great," Luke muttered. "Obviously, it doesn't matter at whose expense. But then the show must go on, so they say."

"I know it wasn't very nice of me. I suppose it's going to make you even angrier when I admit that I kind of got caught up in the whole thing. You seemed so sincere, so earnest. You really made me feel that what happened to me honestly mattered to you. It was pretty romantic for a moment up there."

She flushed slightly, which surprised Luke more than any of her previous responses. He squinted his eyes, reminding himself that Cat was pure Hollywood and this might simply be another great piece of dramatic acting. In fact, he couldn't figure why she was a stunt woman instead of an actress. He'd give her the vote for an Oscar on this performance alone. He stepped back, observing her closely, again wondering what made her tick.

Cat's flush vanished in the wake of her broad smile. "You look like you're about to ask me. 'What's a nice girl like me doing in a job like this?' " she said with a throaty laugh.

Luke grinned. "You're right. Very astute, Miss Roy."

"All the more reason to wonder why I sail out of windows?"

"Right again. I suppose men often ask you that question."

"Actually, the men I know take it for granted. I grew up in the business. I can't remember a time I wasn't working on some stunt or another. I'll bet you I was the only three-year-old in history who knew how to leap off a moving cycle without suffering so much as a scrape."

"I'll bet you're right."

For a moment there was an awkward silence. Neither of them was exactly clear as to why they suddenly felt vulnerable. Maybe it was the look that passed between them, or their awareness of the other's attractiveness; Luke's sensitive, angular, intense good looks; Cat's vibrant, reckless beauty. Something sharply new had occurred. They both felt it.

Cat's gaze returned to the desk. She spotted some travel folders on Greece but drew her attention back to the stack of typewritten papers.

"What is all this writing about?" She kept her tone light, striving to regain her equilibrium. She had already admitted to herself before coming here that she found Luke fascinating and was curious to see him again. But still, her reactions tonight were more intense than she expected. That was not like her.

"I'm working on a book," he said obliquely.

It was the wrong way to answer the question. Cat immediately cocked her head curiously. "What kind of a book?"

Turning slightly, he mumbled, "A manual for sexual fulfillment."

There was no reason on earth to feel awkward about it, he told himself. Sexuality was a vital aspect of life, and of his work with patients. He had given lectures, written erudite papers in prestigious psychiatric journals, and held conferences on sexual problems and ways to achieve a more fulfilling relationship. So why was he feeling so uptight now?

He knew why. For the last twenty minutes or more, his mind had been warring with his body over whether or not to try to seduce the enchantingly delectable Cat Roy. Telling her about his book seemed to him like an admission of just where his thoughts had been this whole time. From the amused yet sultry smile on Cat's face, it was clear that she was having no difficulty reading his mind. She also appeared interested. Or so Luke assumed as he stepped toward her.

Luke had been more accurate in his observation than Cat would have cared to admit. All of a sudden she felt a distinct shift of the tables. For a woman who liked being in the driver's seat, she had just taken a definite tumble toward the backseat!

Playing for time and searching for composure, she picked up one of the travel brochures from the desk. "Greece," she commented with more interest than she felt.

"Yes," Luke concurred, the conversation taking an abrupt turn in the direction of banality. He began to question his observations about Cat's ready seductability. He also questioned the logic of tampering with matters he was not expecting and, if he forced the truth upon himself, not prepared to cope with. To say that they came from opposite ends of the universe would be a strong understatement.

"I'm leaving for Greece in a few weeks—for a couple of months." He was comforted by the impending distance and by having shared the information with her.

Cat's reaction was to feel equally comforted. She liked dealing with all situations in defined time limits—men as well as movies. She liked the thrill, the newness, the excitement of the moment. Then she liked to move on to the next experience or adventure. There was so much out there, Cat sometimes felt like she would never find enough time to do it all.

Besides, she reassured herself as she smiled up at Luke, she was leaving San Francisco in less than ten days, foreseeing no further complications on the shoot—like intriguing, attractive doctors attempting to rescue her in the line of duty. How much trouble could she get into in ten short days?

"I love Greece," Cat said lightly, feeling more secure. "I've done a few films there. Unfortunately, we're always so busy, I rarely get the chance to play tourist." Her eyes swept over the brochure as she had a fleeting fantasy of Luke and her cavorting around ancient ruins under a sultry Greek sun. The image caused her equilibrium to shift yet again. She'd been involved in filming too many love stories lately. She decided to put in for a good horror flick next time.

"Well, I won't be purely a tourist, either," Luke was saying. "I'll be busy working on my book." His voice dropped slightly despite his attempt to sound casual.

"Oh, yes, your book." She smiled. "Sexual freedom . . . right?"

"Fulfillment, sexual fulfillment," he corrected sharply. "It's a manual—a reference book, really—based on my own research as well as others." He emphasized the latter as she lifted her eyes to his in another of her sensually curious gazes.

He coughed. The cause was more discomfort than flu, but when Cat walked off to the kitchen to pour him some more of her secret formula, he was relieved. Those few minutes gave him a chance to reflect on the utter ludicrousness of the situation. What was he, a conservative, low-keyed psychiatrist, doing with this wild and reckless Hollywood spirit? Even in his fantasies he couldn't have come up with a more unlikely match-up.

She handed him the hot drink. This time he didn't resist. Actually, he was beginning to like the way the stuff tasted.

He sat down on the couch. Then standing abruptly, he asked, "What about you? Ah—would you like a drink?"

Cat smiled warmly. "You'd better keep it all. Fortunately, flu bugs keep their distance from me. I can't afford to go into a coughing fit as I'm racing out of a burning building or leaping off an exploding bridge."

"I meant something less medicinal, like a glass of wine or a Scotch. . . ."

He moved over to a small cabinet. Tucking his robe around him more securely, he bent down to inspect his liquor supply. Teri only drank Scotch, and he never did care for more than a glass or two of wine. He also had a few unopened bottles of rye whiskey—gifts from Christmas.

"Wine would be nice."

Luke stood up. "Red or white?"

She joined him at the makeshift bar. An uncorked bottle of red stood on the top. She told him that one looked fine and watched him pour. She liked the way he did things: there was always this subtle hint of sensuality in his movements. She wondered if he knew how sexy she found him. On the surface he presented a picture of the conventional, organized, tidy intellectual—erudite and academically highbrow. He was also sensitive, concerned, empathetic, and gentle. Those qualities were the easy ones to discern. Cat, like Luke, had a knack for seeing beneath the surface. Now she saw a sensually desirable man with a very forceful, provocative presence. She clasped her hands tightly around her drink. She decided she had better swallow it down and get out before she started acting out a scene she was not ready to play. For some mysterious reason, she was having difficulty moving the glass to her lips.

Luke felt suddenly impetuous and slightly giddy. He was quick to deny that it was merely Cat's nearness, idly wondering again if she hadn't put something stronger than seaweed into that drink after all. Whatever the cause, he felt decidedly intoxicated and not in the mood to analyze his feelings. Without a further thought he abruptly turned to Cat, prying the drink from her still tightly clasped hands. Possessively, he slipped his arms around her, his mouth nuzzling the side of her neck. She smelled like fresh daffodils. He kissed her fragrant, silky skin. Her breasts, tight against his chest, heaved deeply. When she drew her head back, he wasted no time capturing that wild, tantalizing mane of hair, tugging her to him for a deep, urgent kiss. Her lips, slightly parted in prepared protest, opened wider as his mouth came down upon hers. His fingers wound through her hair as the kiss deepened.

Cat felt the warmth of his body against her, the urgency of his desire as he gathered her in his arms. She shifted. His grasp tightened. Then she lost herself in the kiss, in the delicious warmth that suffused her. She gave in to her need to respond to him—a need that had begun to take hold hours ago on the ledge outside the window of that fourth-floor apartment.

When they finally parted, Cat was acutely conscious of her own heartbeat and the tightening of her muscles. It was only a kiss, she chided herself, forcing her eyes to meet Luke's. As it turned out, he looked as disturbed and disoriented as she felt. That made her relax.

Smiling, a mischievous twinkle in her dark blue eyes, she shook her hair from her face. "How are you feeling?"

Luke, for all his sophistication and experience with women, actually flushed. And then he grinned. "I feel—very excited," he admitted huskily.

"No, I mean your cold." It was Cat's turn to feel the warm flow of blood return to her cheeks.

Luke laughed. The sound had a nice warm ring to it. "Hey, you know something. I feel a hell of a lot better. I don't know if it was that secret brew of yours or . . ." He intentionally let the sentence drop, tugging her toward him.

She broke the movement with her hands planted flat against his chest.

"It's the medicine," she said a little breathlessly—and a little too emphatically. "Don't let it fool you. You are still a sick guy. Well, now that I've accomplished my mission of mercy, you'd better tuck yourself into bed."

Luke had a much better suggestion, but Cat was already picking up her jacket and hastily making her way to the door. As she reached for the knob, she turned and blew him a kiss.

"I hope I've made up for this morning." Then with one of her crooked little smiles, she placed her cowboy hat jauntily on her head and glided out the door.

Luke nodded. A very pleasant "mission of mercy." He laughed out loud. That understatement had to take the prize for the day.

CHAPTER THREE

The rain had fizzled out. Cat glanced up at the sky, then shifted her gaze to the window ledge that Liz Fuller was stepping out on. The silence grew more intense as camera one zoomed in for a close-up. Cat grinned. She knew how much Liz hated heights, but the actress was a real trooper. There was not a hint of fear in those blue eyes as she glared insolently into the camera, daring anyone to try to stop her.

"Okay, that's a wrap. Nice going, Liz. Harry, help her back inside." Carl Ramsey, the director who had offered Luke that juicy part yesterday, gave a thumbs-up sign and called to Cat to get ready.

Liz walked out of the building and smiled at Cat. At first glance they could have been mistaken for twins. In some ways they were almost too perfectly matched. Their hairstyles were exact duplicates as were their cranberry-colored gowns and thin-strapped heels. Even their rouge and lipstick were the same. Passing each other at the doorway, they exchanged warm smiles.

Close-up, the differences between the two women were obvious. Cat was a good two inches taller than Liz, with dark blue-black eyes and a fuller, more mischievous smile. And while the smaller of the two exuded a sultry kind of glamour, the taller woman had a vivacious, spirited style that was written all over her.

"It's all yours, sweetie," Liz Fuller said affectionately.

"Seems to me we played this scene before." Cat grinned. "Oh, well, it's a nice day for leaping tall buildings. . . ."

Actually, it was a lousy day—gray, chilly, with an intermittent drizzle. Cat and the crew were probably the only group in San Francisco pleased with the bleak lighting. All they prayed for was no downpour until they wrapped up.

"Sorry to do this to you, Cat," the young crewman said apologetically and then turned the hose on her at the entry before she had a chance to hold her breath. She sputtered a bit and shivered for a moment as the cold water blasted her.

"The show must go on," Cat sighed, shaking herself off. She kept a towel around her shoulders until she got upstairs. Dropping it on the floor, she walked to the window, opened it, and stepped outside. There was no hesitation in her move-

41

ments despite the high heels and the narrowness of the ledge. She might have been standing on a terrace checking the weather.

"Over a little to the left." The director motioned her with his hand while he shouted.

Easily, she glided a few more inches away from the window, waiting patiently for the jump signal. There was some kind of difficulty with one of the cameras, so the filming was held up for a couple of minutes.

Her eyes followed the line of windows in the building across the road, coming to rest on Luke's kitchen window.

She smiled to herself, remembering that look on his face when he saw her standing on the ledge yesterday. It was obvious that he had no idea what was really going on. Again she wondered exactly why she had let him believe she was contemplating suicide. She had seen him staring at her from his window, but she knew he probably couldn't tell. Nor could he have made out her half-smile as she saw the frantic upset in his features. She couldn't help smiling at him. He must have thought she was crazy. Then she saw him dash across the street. Surely, he'd notice they were filming. But he had been so disturbed, he'd automatically assumed the cameras were out to capture another San Francisco suicide leap. He'd barged through the crowds and raced to save her.

She was going to tell him the truth right away, but . . .

He was so earnest, so caring, so sincerely

concerned. He was also charming and very attractive. And to top it off, he had a special vulnerable appeal. Maybe it was his miserable cold that made him seem that way, but Cat guessed there was more to it. Anyway, she found herself letting him go on while she played the role he was casting her in. She admitted to herself afterward that it was a cruel thing to do, but she hadn't meant it that way. She had told Luke the truth yesterday. She had gotten carried away, finding herself caught up in their private film—finding herself more than a little attracted to Dr. Luke Eliot.

When she'd looked back up at him after that leap, she knew he was boiling mad. It made matters worse when she grinned. She couldn't help it, though. In the midst of his rage at Carl, he kept coughing and sneezing, and despite the angry set to his face, his eyes still looked stunned by the whole thing.

When he stormed off, Cat found herself debating whether or not to leave well enough alone. When she started back to her hotel, she toyed with the idea of sending Luke a note of apology. No point in going any further than that. So what if she had found him attractive. She had enough complications in her life right now not to go looking for more. And somehow she sensed that Luke Eliot would definitely cause additional complications.

Then she passed that health-food shop. Cat decided it was part fate and a greater part impulsiveness that made her buy the ingredients for the special recipe she had teasingly offered Luke up on that ledge.

She almost threw the stuff out back at her hotel. A dumb idea, she told herself. She certainly had no interest in starting anything. Besides, two people couldn't have gotten off to a poorer start. Not to mention that he wasn't her type and they lived in two totally different worlds.

Cat came up with several more points to her argument on the way to Luke's apartment, but when he opened the door in the middle of a sneezing attack, she forgot about her inner debate. He looked so miserable, so vulnerable. He also looked remarkably attractive in that terry-cloth robe. She let herself be comforted by the fact that he was a sick man and she was merely responding to a budding maternal instinct.

She had underestimated Dr. Luke Eliot's appeal. To make matters worse, she had also underestimated how appealing he found her. This could be trouble with a capital T. When he slipped his arms around her yesterday afternoon, Cat knew it was time to leave. He provoked too many sensations, and she was not looking for a ten-day affair. Or a longer one.

Cat had always been high-spirited and fiercely independent. Her father, who had raised her alone from the time she was three, told her that even as a small child she would tolerate few restrictions. Justin Roy, known by all as Dodger, was one of Hollywood's top stunt men, and as much as he wished Cat wouldn't follow in his footsteps, he knew from the start that he was fighting a losing battle. Cat was fearless and she learned quickly. And like her father, she always had to be on the move. The only thing she ever felt afraid of was being tied down. Professionally, she was heading toward the top of the ladder. Things had not gone so well in her personal life. Maybe she was too caught up with her career, or maybe she always chose the wrong men. Cat kept looking for simple, undemanding relationships that did not interfere with her life-style. Inevitably, all her relationships ended the same way. When the pressure was put on, she made a hasty exit.

When Luke had kissed her yesterday and she had responded so passionately, Cat realized that she was getting in over her head. When she walked out, she had no intention of seeing him again. Her propensity for picking the wrong guy had reached the limit with Luke Eliot.

She was so intent on her thoughts that, although her eyes were unconsciously focused on Luke's window, she almost missed spotting him.

This time there was no look of panic in his expression. In fact, Cat wasn't sure *what* he was feeling. She smiled but couldn't tell if he smiled back or not. Forget it, she ordered herself, forcing her eyes on the director, waiting for the go-ahead signal. Just as he gave it and Cat leaned forward, Luke took a step closer to the window.

She felt the impact of her landing more than she usually did. Too tense. One of the crew helped her off.

He must have seen her wince. "Are you okay?"

"Sure," she said quickly. "You know I'm made of rubber."

He grinned and walked off. Carl called it a wrap and walked over to Cat, giving her an affectionate hug.

"Beautiful job. Monday, all you have to do is jump out of a burning car," he said, kissing her on the cheek.

Cat laughed. "A piece of cake."

A powerfully built man, dark hair streaked with gray, came over to Cat. "Let's see that wrist."

"I'm fine." She stuck her hand behind her back.

Carl's face flashed concern. "What happened, Cat? Did you hurt yourself in that landing?"

"Come on, fellers. All this worry is comforting, but I'm a pro, remember?"

The dark-haired man caught her elbow, pulling her hand from behind and spotting the barely perceptible wince. "Probably only a sprain, but I want it X-rayed. And no lip, Cat." He gave her a piercing look, then eyed Carl Ramsey with the same stare, squashing any lip from either one of them. Before he walked off, he put his arm around Cat, kissed her lightly on the forehead, and smiled with satisfaction, knowing that his orders would be carried out.

"Mount Zion is just a few blocks away. I'll get Harry to zip you over." Carl was already motioning to the burly crewman as he spoke.

Cat shrugged her consent. What choice did she have?

*　*　*

This was another one of those early rising days for Luke, even though it was the start of the weekend. He always scheduled a seven A.M. appointment on Saturdays so that he would be forced to get going at the crack of dawn instead of idling his morning hours away. He'd left the house at six-thirty, spend a difficult fifty-minute hour with a new patient, and was back home before nine.

He had planned to head right over to the university library after his morning appointment. He had even carted his briefcase full of notes with him. When he stepped out of his office, not bothering to open his umbrella against the light drizzle, he changed his mind, deciding to return home instead.

He told himself he ought to go through the new journals he had on his desk before checking out the current reprints at the library. He also told himself that the refilming of the suicide stunt would most likely be cancelled since today it wasn't raining like it had the day before. So much for what Luke Eliot understood about movie magic. Either that, or he was playing mind games with himself, pretending that he had absolutely no interest in seeing Cat Roy leap out of another building.

Sometimes it was a curse being a psychiatrist, he decided. He always saw so easily through his rationalizations. Today was no exception. He was hurrying home on the chance that Cat would be there, that she might stop by his apartment again. She'd left her Thermos there after all. He smiled, thinking how often he told patients who forgot items at his office that it was their way of maintaining a connection with him, as well as a reason to return before their scheduled appointments. He wondered if Cat was aware of that theory. She'd said she was savvy about therapy. Maybe it had even been a conscious maneuver. Cat Roy was not a meek, tentative lady. Luke grinned. This must be his week for understatements.

As he poured himself a cup of coffee and looked out his kitchen window, he had no trouble seeing the makings of a movie. Cables were stretched everywhere. The street was cordoned off with actors dressed as policeman standing duty as a small crowd began to gather. Cameras were moving into place, crewmen and extras scurrying about. He didn't spot Cat at first. Then he saw the window across the road open, a woman in a familiar cranberry gown stepping carefully, hesitantly onto the ledge. Cat's cautious movements surprised him. He drew closer to his window. Staring intently now, he saw his error. It wasn't Cat standing out there. He realized the woman had to be the actress Cat stunted for. He couldn't remember her name. He wasn't much of a moviegoer. An occasional foreign film was about it for him.

He saw Cat then. She was standing in the street, off to the side, watching the woman on the ledge. He caught her smile, immediately wondering what had flashed in her mind, instantly remembering that smile from a much closer vantage point yesterday afternoon. He also vividly remembered the passionate kiss they'd shared. That was something he kept remembering, since he'd watched her fly out of his apartment before he'd had the opportunity to see if the next kiss would have as potent an effect.

Even his rotten cold was better today. Luke was anything but a superstitious fellow; however, he had to admit that Cat Roy had had an amazing effect on his flu as well as his body. He figured it would be safer to think it was that crazy brew rather than the woman herself who had produced the miracle cure, but he couldn't get himself to believe it. No, there was definitely something about Cat. . . .

He shook his head free of the direction in which his thoughts were heading. This is ridiculous, he scolded himself. When he was seventeen, he'd fallen madly in love with Sophia Loren after seeing her in *Divorce Italian Style*, a lusty Italian film. For months he'd fantasized what it would be like to spend a night with that dark-haired, voluptuous beauty. For months he'd made disappointing comparisons between his high school girl friends and the sexy actress. Now, after all those years of growing up and learning the difference between fantasy and reality, he was regressing to his adolescence all over again. His thoughts about Cat were not far removed from those he'd secretly coveted twenty years ago about Sophia. She was always simply Sophia in his fantasies.

Okay, so maybe it wasn't quite the same. He'd never swept the Italian actress in his arms, passionately kissing those soft ruby lips. He'd never exchanged sensual smiles with Sophia. He'd never been offered a taste of elixir . . .

Elixir! Yesterday it was a godawful brew. Today it was elixir. You're really slipping, Eliot, he warned himself. He started to walk away from the window. Then he heard the voice of the guy who'd offered to put his name in lights—or at least in the long list of extras—call Cat's name. She waved back to the director. Luke thought she was about to look up at his window, but instead she walked over to the entry of the building, pausing for a couple of minutes to talk with her near look-alike. One of the crewmen, carrying a garden hose in his hand, joined Cat as the other actress walked away. Cat hadn't looked up at Luke once since he'd spotted her. Was she intentionally avoiding him, or had she lost interest? Was yesterday a brief lark to share a few laughs over with her rugged, robust Hollywood friends?

He felt a momentary satisfaction as he watched her get doused with the water from the hose. It quickly faded, replaced by a flash of arousal as he observed the shape of her slender body outlined by the clinging wet gown. She wasn't Sophia Loren, but Luke's tastes had changed since adolescence. Cat Roy had all the right measurements for his adult interest. He took a swallow of lukewarm coffee.

A minute later he watched her step out on the ledge. She moved with a confident, natural grace that was truly impressive. Imagining himself in her place, Luke would have been more than a little nervous. Again he wondered what made Cat Roy tick. She never did answer his question about what she was doing in a job like this. And yet, he realized, the profession fit her. She had this fearless, spirited quality that seemed a basic part of her nature. Luke both admired that quality as well as found it dangerous. Dangerous for her—and for him.

Their eyes met across the distance. Cat smiled. He didn't smile back. His mind was too flooded with sensations. He quickly glanced down at the ground, making sure the inflatable mattresses were in place. This time he knew it was a movie and that Cat was performing a stunt she had probably done a hundred times. The panic he felt yesterday was no longer present. And yet, he unconsciously held his breath, feeling a knot tighten in his stomach. What if she missed those mattresses?

He stepped closer to the window as she leaned forward. How could she so blithely let herself go? How could he stand by watching her? He shuddered as he saw her land, letting out a deep breath of relief as she swung over to the side of the mattress. This was not for him. Still, he kept staring as the director walked over to her. He couldn't hear her laughter, but he had not forgotten the sound from yesterday. Then he spied a ruggedly handsome man come up to Cat and grab her. Rather roughly, Luke thought, feeling the muscles in his jaw tighten. Spotting Cat's scowl increased his irritation at the guy. The anger switched to a stab of jealousy as the man put his arm around Cat, kissing her in a way that Luke decided was distinctly possessive.

He moved away from the window, pouring his now cold coffee into the sink. He had to get a grip on himself before he went completely nuts. The sooner he forgot about Cat Roy and her wild stunts, the better he was going to feel. As if to reinforce that thought, he broke into a coughing fit. So much for magical cures.

"I thought you weren't going to show. You're never late." Teri Caulfield placed her glass of Scotch back on the Mexican tile-topped table.

"Sorry." Luke slid into a seat across from Teri and smiled. "I'm haven't been myself for the last couple of days." Those understatements just kept rolling along.

Teri's sharply etched features registered concern. A small furrow appeared across her brow. Luke never noticed before that her frown gave her a slightly puckered look. He hurried to assure her he was fine—just a touch of flu.

"You should have stopped at the office. Are you sure you feel up to lunch?"

"Come on, Teri. This is supposed to be a friendly date, not a medical consultation. I'm feeling terrific now. Hardly a sniffle left in me. And I'm starving." He found himself irritated at her continued close inspection.

The truth was he almost hadn't shown up this afternoon. He had called Teri's office fifteen minutes ago, hoping to catch her in, so that he could cancel out on their luncheon. When the answering service had said she'd left for the day, he considered calling the restaurant to leave a message for her, but then he decided that the wisest thing to do was to keep the date. He really needed to touch base with reality again in his determined efforts to get Cat Roy off his mind. In a way, feeling so much better physically wasn't helping. He was back to thinking Cat might have magic powers at that.

"How's the book coming?" Teri asked in her twangy New England accent.

Luke shrugged. He and Teri often discussed his research and the work on his book. Unlike when Cat brought up the subject, Teri's question did not generate embarrassing fantasies. "I picked up an interesting article the other day by Franz Hellman about achievement and sexual inhibitions. You'll have to read it when you get a chance."

Teri gave him an odd look. He hadn't meant anything personal by the remark. He tried for a warm smile, but it didn't quite come off. He was annoyed at himself, annoyed at Teri, annoyed that Cat Roy kept flitting into his mind. And he was most annoyed at the constant comparisons he found himself making between Teri and Cat.

Teri was certainly an attractive woman, but there was an archness in her manner that Luke found particularly noticeable today. He was annoyed by her almost too perfect application of makeup, her meticulously coordinated Ralph Lauren skirt and sweater, and the crisp, twangy accent that gave her a thick Harvard University aura. These were the qualities, he reminded himself, that had first attracted him to Teri Caulfield. He liked the air of success and aristocratic good looks she exuded. He liked her intellectual bent, her controlled emotionalism. She was bright, accomplished, interesting, and undemanding. And she could not have been more unlike Cat Roy in every conceivable way.

That was the problem. Teri fit a comfortable mold that Luke readily understood and related to. Cat Roy fit no mold at all. That was the heart of his fascination with her. She was unique, captivating, wholly unpredictable, and utterly sensual. He couldn't keep his mind off his fantasies of her for more than five seconds at a stretch. He also managed to keep evading his own question of how a sophisticated, intelligent man—a psychiatrist no less—could sink to such blatant, primitive infatuation.

"You haven't heard a word I said," Teri scolded him lightly.

"Sorry. My mind is still on that pile of journals on my desk," he lied. It wasn't like him to fabricate stories. He was tempted to tell Teri about Cat but changed his mind. She would tell him in no uncertain terms that he needed to have his head examined. Physician, heal thyself. He grinned.

"Luke Eliot, what is the matter with you? First you look like you're a million miles away, and then you're laughing to yourself over some obviously private joke. Did you take something stronger than aspirin for that cold?"

Elixir, he thought. "No, of course not," he answered her. "You know I don't like drugs."

"I know that you're acting strange today. It's a good thing you're going to Greece in a few weeks. You need a rest." She smiled across at him, reaching for his hand. "I'm going to miss you, though."

Teri was at her prettiest when she smiled. Her hazel eyes crinkled nicely at the corners, her pale skin reflected a faint rosy hue, her delicate lips curved up gracefully. She shook her head slightly as Luke smiled back. A whisk of blond hair escaped her sophisticated chignon. She tucked it carefully back into place.

The gesture ruined the pleasant effect her smile had generated. The memory of Cat's wild mane tumbling haphazardly around her face as she removed that cowboy hat came into clear focus again. Luke picked up the menu and tried to concentrate on food. It wasn't easy. He had also lied to Teri when he'd said he was starving. He had no appetite at all.

Luke followed Teri's lead, ordering the same roast beef on croissant, French fries, and salad. He managed some small talk while they waited for the food to arrive, but mostly he let Teri carry the conversation.

"Todd Archer called the other day. He's going to be in town for the conference tomorrow, and I said we'd save a seat for him. He's looking forward to Brodie's paper on the psychological effects of over-the-counter medications. I'm eager to hear his findings on that myself," Teri said, refusing another Scotch when the waiter brought over their sandwiches. "I guess you're more interested in Matheson's work about the effects of tranquilizers on sexual responsiveness."

Luke bit into his roast beef sandwich and nodded. Swallowing, he said, "I talked with Matheson a couple of months ago about his research. Very impressive. Actually, there are a few good people presenting tomorrow. We should both enjoy it."

Luke felt better. He had no trouble picturing Teri as his date at the medical conference tomorrow. She fit in perfectly, and he was confident that they both would have a good time. He could not imagine someone like Cat Roy sitting beside him as Fleisher discussed the interrelationships of psychopharmacology and psychoanalysis, or when Chester Brodie reported his findings on the emotional aspects of abusing cough syrup and nose spray. And she would probably laugh in that throaty, utterly sensual way of hers when Matheson got down to a discussion of Valium and its repercussions on sexual potency. He was increasingly glad that he had kept this luncheon date with Teri after all. The comforting realities were slowly but surely beginning to edge out his disturbing fantasies.

Things were moving along nicely until a large group of people walked into the restaurant and crowded around a nearby booth. Luke recognized several of them, but one in particular caught his eye. Fantasy, in the form of a dynamite-looking, dark-haired stunt woman, instantly disrupted Luke Eliot's carefully garnered, renewed grip on reality.

CHAPTER FOUR

Cat's hair was still damp from the morning's impro-
vised shower. A few dark strands curled against
her cheek. She was dressed in the same suede
cowboy jacket as yesterday afternoon, with a pair
of tight blue jeans clinging to her sleek body.

Luke's ever observant eye took in the details
before Cat turned in his direction and saw him.
Their eyes held for a moment, Cat's a bit startled
at seeing him so unexpectedly, Luke's warmly
appreciative.

She brushed a wayward strand of hair from
her cheek. Luke's eyes rested on the Ace bandage wound around her wrist. His expression
showed concern. Cat's gaze moved across the table
to Teri. Her expression registered a shadow of
disappointment.

She hesitated. Luke could see her chest heave

as she took in a deeper breath. He smiled. Cat walked over to him.

"Hi, Doc. How are you feeling today?" She looked him straight in the eye, flashing a winning smile.

"Better. Much better."

"You look better." She grinned. "Amazing what a good night's rest can do for a person."

"What about you?" Luke asked, pointing to her bandaged wrist. He caught Teri's puzzled expression but ignored it for the moment.

"Oh, this. Nothing. Just a slight sprain. Pitfalls on the trade." Cat's smile took in Luke and his companion.

Luke made the introductions as the two women eyed each other with curiosity.

"Nice to meet you, Miss Caulfield." Cat extended her hand.

"Dr. Caulfield," Teri corrected, briefly shaking hands. "I hope you've had that wrist checked. Sometimes what feels like a mere sprain could be a small fracture."

Cat nodded, taking in the "Doctor," the twangy voice, and Teri Caulfield's young Joan Kennedy look and manner. Cat knew her immediate dislike of the woman had nothing to do with status, locale, or politics. It had to do with the fact that Dr. Caulfield was with Luke Eliot. She was annoyed at the streak of jealousy that went through her.

"Cat is doing some stunts for a film they're shooting across from my apartment house," Luke explained, intentionally not going into the embarrassing details of their actual first encounter.

Cat picked up the hint. "Yes, I met Luke when he was watching us . . . do some action shots."

"That must be a fascinating line of work. As well as a risky one."

"I tend to find that most exciting things have risks attached. That's part of what makes them exciting, I guess. Anyway, I'm reasonably careful, and I never take foolish chances."

Teri's appraisal narrowed before she turned her head to Luke.

"Miss Roy would make an interesting study, don't you think, Luke? You've probably already been formulating some theories." To Cat, Teri added, "Luke has a sharply analytic mind—always trying to figure out the reasons behind people's actions."

"You mean what makes someone tick," she murmured, a flicker of a smile on her lips. "Yes, Luke does have a questioning mind."

"Pitfalls of the trade," Luke echoed. "But only with patients." He shot Teri a scowl.

"Then I don't have to worry—if we should meet again sometime—about having my actions analyzed."

When she met Luke's gaze this time, her eyes were a sparkling blue-green. So they did change color with her mood. He found this particular shade especially ravishing. Fantasies started crowding his mind again.

"Well—uh—it was nice running into you again,

Luke. And nice to meet you, too, Dr. Caulfield. I should get back to my friends." She turned to leave.

Luke collected his wits as she started off. "Cat . . ."

She looked back at him.

"Thanks." There was a definite twinkle in his eyes. The message in them was clear. Cat knew he appreciated her skipping the details of their encounter. She smiled. It had not all been to save Luke's face. She admitted a private enjoyment out of keeping Dr. Caulfield guessing.

Her smiled broadened as she heard Luke's explanation to Teri.

"Cat had some terrific—uh, cough syrup that she let me try. It—it was very effective."

"Obviously."

Luke bit into his croissant. Teri looked over at Cat.

"She's stunning. And a little kooky, don't you think? Very Hollywood." Teri hoped her tone was light. She had been dating Luke for nearly a year. In all that time she had been satisfied to keep the relationship very casual and could not recall one prior instance when she felt such a rush of jealousy. After all, it wasn't as if she and Luke were emotionally tied up with one another. They saw each other a couple of times a month, mostly to attend conventions and functions that required escorts. Sometimes, like today, they met for a friendly lunch and brought each other up to date on what they were doing. She liked Luke, enjoyed his company, certainly found him attractive, but she had only been in private practice a couple of years, and most of her energy had been directed toward her work. Now, for the first time, she wondered if she hadn't taken her involvement with Luke too casually. She had to admit that she found his overtly appreciative survey of Cat Roy more than a little irritating. She motioned the waiter over and ordered a second Scotch.

Luke bristled at Teri's remarks about Cat being Hollywood and kooky, but he did not want to come across defensively. He stuck with her first statement. "Yes, she is striking-looking. Exotic almost."

"Uhm. Her pupils were slightly dilated. Did you notice?" Teri's tone was markedly professional.

"No."

She shrugged. "I'd put an educated bet on cocaine. That's the current popular Hollywood drug."

Luke forgot about sounding defensive. "She doesn't use cocaine—or any other drugs for that matter. She's a vegetarian."

"Oh. Well, then, I guess I'm wrong. What else do you know about her?" She didn't bother to keep her tone light this time. So what if Luke knew she was a little jealous? Maybe it was time to reevaluate the status of their relationship. It would be nice to see Luke Eliot survey her with that hint of warm seduction for a change.

"Not much," Luke responded, hearing the arch tone in his voice. He did not particularly like the switch in Teri's manner. He had no interest in altering the status quo.

"I can't imagine doing those crazy stunts," Teri commented. "I don't care what she says, the risks are enormous. You read about horrible accidents all the time when they're doing stunts in films—"

"Can we get off the topic?" Luke interrupted. His thoughts had not been all that different from Teri's about the dangers of Cat's profession, but it was a subject that he found too disturbing to dwell on.

"Sorry. Just making conversation."

The film crew was more boisterous than the rest of the patrons in the restaurant. Teri determinedly ignored them, but Luke, whose back was to Cat, kept picking up the sound of her voice and her throaty laugh.

"Are you going back to your office this afternoon?" Luke asked, finishing his sandwich.

Teri cocked her head. "I really should. I've got a pile of medical reports sitting on my desk."

Luke nodded.

"I could be persuaded to let them go another day. . . ."

"Well, I still have those journals to tackle. Getting sick put me way off my schedule."

"Sometimes I wonder if the two of us aren't too well organized." Actually, she hadn't wondered about it before today.

"If I didn't keep to a regimen I might never get anything done. Behind this facade of well-controlled order lurks the heart of an impulsive devil."

63

"You're full of surprises today, Dr. Eliot. And all this time I thought I knew you so well."

Luke swept the napkin off his lap, wiped his lips, and placed the cloth on the table. "Sometimes I even surprise myself." He got up from his chair, walked around to pull out Teri's seat, and glanced over at Cat.

She was talking to a young body-beautiful guy, but she must have felt Luke's eyes on her. She turned her head toward him. When Teri bent to retrieve her purse, Cat winked, a wide grin making her look all the more dazzling.

He took Teri's arm as he guided her around Cat's table. Okay, Luke, he thought, you've had your moment of fantasy. Wave good-bye and get back to reality.

He coughed just as he got to Cat.

She looked up over her shoulder. "Take care of that cold, Doc," she said in her low, husky voice.

Sophia Loren had never sounded that good. Or stirred fantasies as vivid.

He opened the door for Teri, stepped outside after her, and took three steps before coming to a sudden stop.

"Hold on one sec, Teri. I . . . I forgot something."

He didn't wait for her response, swerving back around and through the restaurant door again before Teri realized what was happening.

He strode over to Cat's table. Her blue eyes—pure sea-blue now and glittering with pleasure—met his.

"I was wondering where you were staying in

64

town, in case I need some more of that medicine of yours." The others at the table grew silent, but he ignored them completely.

So did Cat. "I'm at the Ambassador."

He nodded, a slow smile appearing on his lips as he caught the warm sparkle in her eyes.

His smile lasted all the way to the front door. It faded when a large, good-looking older man walked past him and over to Cat's table. It was the same guy who had been all over Cat on the set. Okay, so maybe he was exaggerating, he told himself. He stopped arguing the point when he saw the man bend over Cat and give her a very affectionate hug. What disturbed him the most was the tender look in Cat's eyes as she returned the embrace. Then she reached over and handed the man a paper bag of food. He kissed her again, waved to everyone else at the table, and headed back toward the door. Luke hurried through it first.

"Did you find what you'd forgotten?" Teri asked as Luke stepped back outside.

"No," he said gruffly. "I must have made a mistake."

"Pass the mustard, Cat."

Cat picked up the salt shaker and slid it across the table.

"Mustard, not salt. Wake up, Cat. Who's that guy, anyway?"

Ben Seaton, the stunt man sitting next to Cat, snickered. "That's no guy. He's Cat's knight in shining armor. Right, Cat?" He speared a French fry as he waited for her response.

She stirred her tea absently, a glimmer of a smile on her lips.

Joanie Weston, the special effects assistant who had asked Cat for the mustard, laughed. "Oh, so that's the guy who tried to save you from suicide yesterday. That had to be one of the funniest—"

"Stop it, both of you," Cat scolded lightly, casting her big blue eyes around the table in warning. "I don't think it was in the least bit funny. It was—it was quite gallant, romantic, and . . ." Her eyes sparkled. "Okay, it was a little funny, too. But Luke Eliot happens to be a very renowned psychiatrist and he was acting on a—a professional instinct."

"That wasn't professional instinct I saw in those sexy eyes of his a minute ago." Joanie grinned. "And all this time I thought most psychiatrists looked like Sigmund Freud. Do you think your Dr. Eliot takes short-term patients?" she teased.

"He's not *my* doctor," Cat retorted, grabbing the plastic container of mustard. "Here, go drown your hot dog."

"You're beginning to make me jealous, Cat," Ben murmured with a seductive grin. "You're not falling for that guy, are you? He's definitely not your type. You get yourself tangled up with a shrink and in no time he'll have you so well analyzed that you'll never jump out another window again."

66

"That's ridiculous, Ben." Cat picked up her broccoli quiche and took a large bite.

"Which part? He's not for you, or he won't keep you from leaping?"

She shot him a wide grin. "Figure it out for yourself."

The rest of the group laughed, except for Ben. This was the fourth picture he had been on with Cat, and he had been trying unsuccessfully through all of them to get somewhere with her. So far he hadn't made it to first base, but he wasn't ready to give up hope. He focused his attention on his chicken sandwich, deciding that this Eliot wasn't a real threat. The thought of the doctor and Cat as a pair was not only improbable, it was downright funny. No, he told himself, Cat would never get involved with a straight-arrow, conservative dude like that. She had to be pulling everyone's leg.

Cat nibbled on her French fries, her mind in the same place as Ben's. Only she was not having the same thoughts. She was recalling Luke Eliot's warm, sexy eyes, the rich timbre of his voice, the way he smiled when she told him the name of her hotel. She was certain he would contact her, and the expectation of meeting him again gave her a shiver of anticipation.

There had been a hint of promise in their shared smile. Cat wasn't sure exactly what that promise was, but right now she didn't feel like figuring it out. She liked the rush of excitement she was experiencing, the funny tingling sensation in the pit of her stomach, the slightly dizzy feeling coursing through her.

Liz Fuller walked into the restaurant and joined the others at the large booth. She looked less like Cat now, with her dark hair swept up into a coiled knot, large sunglasses covering those baby-blue eyes, her stage makeup removed to reveal a much paler complexion. Her gestures and movements were different, too. They were more contained and controlled than the woman who risked life and limb for her. There was a quiet hush in the restaurant as people began to recognize the actress, then a bustle of activity and whispers. Several people came over for autographs, which Liz signed graciously.

Ben Seaton got up and offered the star his seat.

"Your throne, Miss Fuller," he teased playfully. "Don't get writer's cramp, now. You still have some scenes to shoot this afternoon." He grinned broadly, flexing a bicep. "See you later, gang. I have to get back and beat up Liz's lover—for the twenty-fifth time. If we do one more retake, I think I'll have to throw a few real punches—at Carl."

"Don't you dare." Liz laughed. "Carl is a gem of a director, and I want him to stay in one piece for the next week and a half and finish this little farce on schedule. I have other fish to fry when this piece of fluff is wrapped up." Her eyes gleamed with mysterious pleasure.

Cat watched Liz as she sat down and ran a well-manicured finger along the menu. Then she looked over at Cat's half-eaten quiche.

"God, that's disgusting. How can you eat all of those revolting calories and stay so gorgeously thin?"

"It's amazing the number of calories you use up tumbling off bridges and out of windows."

"I think I'll keep my feet on the ground and order the fruit salad plate."

The waitress, waiting with bated breath in the wings, scurried over to Liz when the actress put down her menu. The young woman immediately asked the star for her autograph. Liz graciously signed the cardboard back of the sales slip book and then gave her order, flashing the waitress one of her best theatrical smiles.

Cat laughed. "I bet you get two cherries on top of your cottage cheese for that. I'll take crashing motorcycles and burning buildings to autograph seekers anytime."

"They only get to me on my bad days. Don't forget—they're the ones who buy the movie tickets. By the way, speaking of crashing motorcycles and burning buildings," Liz said, switching gears as she so often did, "my agent called before I came over here to tell me that he was completing negotiations for Peter Whitney's new film, *Victims*. I read the script last month and it's a knockout. It means leaving next Friday for a few weeks on location in Rome. Which unfortunately means a few weeks fighting off the temptations of pasta, vino, and beautiful Italian men. But it's a very juicy part that I am dying to sink my pearly white teeth into, and Peter Whitney did help Carrie Morgan win that Oscar last year."

Liz closed her eyes for a moment, her long black lashes fluttering over her high cheekbones. "This is my year, Cat. I feel it in my blood." She opened her eyes and grinned. "The cry of the unrewarded."

"There's an Oscar up there with your name on it," Cat said, laughing. "I feel it in my blood."

Liz patted Cat's hand affectionately. "I adore you even though you torment me with mouth-watering quiche. Want to come along to Roma? I'm sure Whitney would love to have you stunt for me if you have nothing else lined up yet. What do you say? Shall I put in the word?"

Cat looked over at Liz thoughtfully. "I don't know. I was thinking about a film Walt Logan is doing this summer, but I haven't gotten back to him yet. They're going to be shooting most of the stunts in and around Mexico City."

"Tacos when you could have fettuccine? Cat, how could you even consider Logan when Italy beckons?"

"Is Italy 'it' for location shots?"

"Where else would you like to go?"

Cat grinned, shrugging her shoulders. "I hear the Greek islands are nice this time of year. The thought of lolling around sandy Aegean beaches on my days off does have definite appeal over tacos and *turista*."

"Now that you mention it," Liz said, "I think Peter is going to do a few days' work in Greece. In fact, there were some notations in my script about Crete and a couple of other little islands. Actually,

70

one of them was a place I visited a few years back when I was dating Tony Vargos and we took that fabulous cruise along the islands in that absolutely sumptuous yacht of his. Did I tell you he had to sell it last year? After that string of flops he had, the poor guy was forced to get rid of the boat, sublet his villa in Spain, and last time I saw him, he was driving around in a very used-looking Porsche instead of that silver Jag he loved so much."

"Which island?"

"Huh? Oh, right. How did I get off on the Vargos tangent?"

"Maybe you really liked the man," Cat offered.

Liz pursed her lips. "He was stunning—and quite charming. Nothing like the gossip mongers tout. But then, who is? If I believed everything that was written about me, I would have thrown a few punches of my own by now. Poor Tony. God, this is a crazy business. What are we doing in it, Cat?"

"Having fun, of course." She smiled broadly. "And filling up our bankbooks."

"True." Liz laughed. "Anyway, Skiathos is the name of the island where Tony and I . . ." She didn't bother finishing the sentence. Instead she lifted the tall glass of Perrier to her lips and took a long sip. She smiled across at Cat, whose expression had become suddenly mysterious. "Do you know the island?"

"I've heard of it," Cat said, stretching her long legs under the table. "I read something about it just recently." In Luke Eliot's apartment to be

71

exact. One of the brochures she had picked up from his desk was all about the glories of the Sporades islands off the Greek mainland. Skiathos appeared in bright red lettering on the front cover.

"So, what do you say? Do you want to fight killer sharks in the aqua Mediterranean, fall off a couple of cliffs, and get into a few crashes for me? I know of at least one glorious triple-car smash-up in the script, and there's sure to be lots more fun and games on this one, knowing dear Peter's penchant for that kind of thing."

"Unfortunately, I have a couple of pals in the business who've stunted for him and barely lived to tell about it. Peter sometimes gets a little carried away with his notions of what kinds of stunts are humanly possible."

"Don't worry. Lenny told me Peter is going to try to get your father to supervise. Dodger is cautious enough to keep Peter Whitney in line. And he's particularly careful about his little girl."

"Too careful, sometimes." Cat sighed. "Dodger's getting more finicky with age." She popped the last piece of quiche into her mouth. "There should be some interesting fireworks between Dodger and dear old Peter if my dad takes this one on."

"Come along and watch them, then."

"I'll have to think about it," Cat mused, a fleeting fantasy of Luke stretched out on glistening white Aegean sand crossing her mind. Yes, she thought, it was definitely something to consider. Maybe after this evening, she would be ready to let Liz know her decision.

*   *   *

Luke tried to settle into his work. After spending a good twenty minutes sharpening pencils, organizing the books and papers on his desk into neat stacks, and changing the perfectly serviceable ribbon on his typewriter, he finally admitted to himself that his mind was not going to cooperate with the work he had set out to do. Scowling, he slammed a book shut and rubbed his eyes.

He reached for his phone and dialed his answering service for any messages. There was only one—from Max Hart, Luke's former supervisor and current friend and mentor. The message asked Luke to call back but indicated that there was no emergency.

It had been several years since Luke had felt a pressing need to talk with Max about any personal issues. When Luke had first gone into practice, Max had been very supportive, as well as remarkably sensitive and understanding to Luke's concerns about leaving his safe niche at San Francisco General. Max had helped Luke realize the importance of testing new ground and of taking worthwhile risks.

Luke stared at the phone for a few moments. What would Max say if he told him he had been contemplating getting mixed up with a wildly beautiful Hollywood stunt woman? What would he say about this absurd streak of jealousy that had suddenly materialized? How would he interpret the fantasies that kept bombarding him? Luke wasn't sure if he wanted to hear the answers to those questions, but he began dialing Max's number, anyway.

The line was busy. Luke wandered into the kitchen. The Thermos that Cat had brought over yesterday afternoon was tipped upside down on the drainboard. He walked over and lifted it up. A few drops of water splashed onto his hand. There was still a faint aroma of chicory. He ran it under the tap again. The scent was still there, clinging, just as his thoughts about Cat clung to his mind. He studied the Thermos. I should return it to her, he thought. Maybe she has some other missions of mercy. . . .

He redialed Max Hart's number, getting a ring this time. The Thermos was still in his hand as Max said hello. Luke bent down and slid the container into the cupboard under the sink.

"Hello, Max."

"Luke. You didn't have to hurry to call back. I just wanted to let you know I saw that Mr. Miller you referred."

"Oh. That's good. He's—uhm—one of those people who have trouble coping with success."

"And women. He told me he always chooses the wrong ones."

"Sounds familiar."

"Yes. We both see that symptom enough," Max agreed. "So Luke, how are you? You sound like you have a cold."

"I've—I've been fighting something off for the past few days." Luke's eyes drifted to the cupboard door. "It's funny you should bring up Miller.

74

I just saw this man—a patient," Luke emphasized, "who has become infatuated with this woman. She's kind of reckless, a little kooky maybe. Totally different type than—than this patient. He's quite perceptive about the problem. Realizes it's ridiculous to let himself get carried away. But he's constantly having to fight off these fantasies—very vivid ones. Can't get this woman off his mind, in fact."

"Ah, obsessive," Max mused.

"No. No, I wouldn't go that far," Luke balked. "I mean, this woman does sound very appealing. Very appealing." A few beads of perspiration broke out on Luke's brow.

"I see."

There was a pause. Max spoke first. "So, tell me, Luke. How did you deal with this situation?"

"Well, I tried to get him to realize it was probably a temporary feeling—a brief infatuation. You meet a strikingly stunning, tempestuous woman—a lovely, free spirit—and it's natural to feel an attraction, a desire. Why wouldn't you have fantasies, a longing to see her again?"

"I can't imagine any reason why not," Max said in his most analytic voice.

"Right. That's what I told him."

"Good."

Again, there was a brief silence.

"So, Luke, when do I get to meet this stunning, tempestuous spirit of yours?"

Luke laughed. "I'm becoming an old fool before my time, Max. Tell me, do you think I'm crazy?"

"My friend, all I can answer is that without a little bit of madness where would you and I be? I will admit something to you, Luke. I worry more about those people who are too sane than those with a little touch of craziness in their soul."

"Now I know how my patients feel when I fend off direct questions." Luke sighed. "But I get the point, Max. I just have to figure out what to do about it."

76

CHAPTER FIVE

"How does it feel?" Joanie Weston asked, stepping back after adjusting the metal harness.

"Terrific. I feel like a horse being taken off to the glue factory." Cat smirked, slipping on the tweed suit jacket.

Carl strode over with Tim Ryan, the head of special effects. "Okay, Cat. This one is simple enough. Take five steps toward the car, left hand poised to open the front door, then *bang*. Just remember, when the shot comes and that contraption you're wired to jerks you slightly backward, you clutch the door handle, then slowly let your hand slide down the side of the car to the pavement." He turned to Ryan. "Don't give her too violent a tug or she won't be able to reach that handle."

Ryan nodded to Carl and then came up closer to Cat, slipping his hand under her jacket.

"Fresh." She grinned.

"Wouldn't I love to be," he teased back, making sure the rubber sacs of "blood" were securely taped over the tiny, flat pieces of metal squibs containing explosive and secured to the metal plate of Cat's vest. When the gunshot went off, Ryan would electrically detonate the squibs to duplicate the impact of a real bullet. He would also pull the wire on the spring-operated harness around Cat's waist to yank the wounded woman backward, effectively creating the realistic movement of being hit. It was one of the more routine stunts, but nevertheless, it had to be carefully checked out so that everything was perfectly synchronized.

"We're all set," Ryan called over to Carl.

"Never let it be said I wouldn't die for you, Tim," Cat whispered before he returned to his switches and wires.

Everything went like clockwork, and Cat was relieved they wouldn't have to do another take. It was close to four o'clock and she wanted to stop at Dina's, a small boutique on Union Street she'd passed when she'd gone to lunch that afternoon. There was a gorgeous, slinky red taffeta dress in the window, shimmering and done up with a wild combination of ruffles and ribbons. It was totally outrageous, and Cat found it irresistibly sinful—the perfect getup to greet Luke's arrival tonight.

She bought the dress without blinking an eye at the price tag. Wild outfits were one of her occasional weaknesses. She adored costumes—from cowgirl togs to tiaras—and she had the panache to carry off whatever look she was in the mood for.

She stopped at the desk in the lobby of the Ambassador Hotel.

"Any messages for me?"

The clerk, a gaunt young man who was still suffering from an extended case of acne, slipped a folded paper out of her mail slot. He eyed her appreciatively as he handed her the note.

She read it and then looked back up at the clerk. "No other messages—or calls?"

He double-checked her box and shook his head.

Cat shrugged. Luke might have some late-afternoon patients or be working on his book. She smiled, remembering the flush of embarrassment on his face when he'd told her he was writing about sexual fulfillment. As she rode up in the elevator to the seventh floor, she found herself wondering about the extent of Luke Eliot's personal research for that book. Was Dr. Teri Caulfield one of his willing subjects? She shifted the shopping bag from Dina's to her other hand. Why did she buy the dress, anyway? "Just what are your intentions toward this doctor, Miss Roy?" she whispered out loud in the empty elevator. She couldn't come up with an answer. All she knew was that Luke Eliot triggered responses and fantasies in her that she could not ignore.

There was more than a physical attraction here, although that certainly was a prominent feature. But there was something else. She had felt it right from the start—a special communication. *Simpatico*.

That was it. With all the differences she could list between them, there was an invisible thread that seemed to connect them.

Her hand trembled slightly as she unlocked the door to her room. She chided herself for getting too carried away with fantasies. This wasn't a movie. There wasn't going to be any pat Hollywood finale. In real life, endings could be tough to take. It was rare for Cat to shy away from danger, but she began to wonder if this was one time the risks would be too great. She had a gut feeling that Luke Eliot was going to disrupt her life more than anyone else ever had.

The phone rang. She immediately forgot her reservations as she ran to answer it.

"Oh, Ben."

"Don't sound so excited."

Neither of them tried to mask the disappointment in their voices.

"I just got in," Cat said.

"How did things go after I left?"

"Routine. I only had to get shot at once."

Ben laughed. "It isn't fair. Carl decided, after the twenty-fifth brawl with Owen, that he wants to rework the whole fight. Thank God tomorrow's Sunday and I get a day to recuperate before learning the new choreography."

"About tonight, Ben . . ."

"Don't turn me down, Cat. A guy can handle just so much rejection. Besides, haven't I gotten knocked down enough for one day?"

"You're a pro. You know how to move with the punches."

"That one went right to the solar plexus, babe." Ben sighed. "When are you going to discover that the two of us are made for each other?"

Cat glanced over at the red taffeta dress she had extracted from the shopping bag and spread over her bed. Ben was giving her the perfect place to wear it—a party one of his friends was throwing over at Frauley's, a swank new dinner club in the Embarcadero.

If Luke didn't show up she might not get to wear that dress for a while. She'd have to take the risk.

Ben managed to handle the rejection gracefully enough. Cat didn't doubt that he would try again. She wondered how Luke would interpret her lack of interest in Ben Seaton. Ben was as virile and attractive as the handsome stars he stunted for; he seemed to be crazy about Cat, warmly attentive and sensual. They shared the same profession, some of the same interests. Yet there had never been any sparks. Then Cat remembered Luke emphasizing that he only analyzed patients.

When an hour went by and there was still no word from Luke, Cat began to get tense. She covered her disappointment with irritation. Why had he asked her where she was staying, anyway? Luke hadn't impressed her as the kind of man who played games, but maybe she had misread him.

She should never have stopped in that health-food store. She should never have started her crazy flirtation up on that ledge. She should chalk up the whole experience as a funny episode to tell her grandchildren one day. Most of all, she should stop staring at her bedside phone willing it to ring again.

Cat never could tolerate waiting for things to happen. She switched on the radio, found a noisy rock station, and began doing some rigorous aerobics. Then, having worked up a good sweat, she took a shower. When she walked back into the bedroom, she hesitated before walking over to the telephone again.

He might have phoned while she was in the bathroom. She dialed the clerk. No calls. The white terry-cloth towel fell to the carpet as she slipped on her robe. She walked over to the bed and sat down, carelessly shoving the red dress aside. She leaned back against the pillows, letting her long legs slide over the red taffeta. Rational thoughts about this being all for the best mingled with her disturbingly sensual fantasies.

Her irritation won out over her good sense. Reaching for the phone directory on the shelf of the end table, she turned to the *E*s. Luke's home number wasn't listed. It made sense that he would not want patients indiscriminately calling him at his house. She dialed the listed office exchange.

"Dr. Luke Eliot's office." The voice was nasal and feminine.

"Is this Dr. Eliot's secretary?"

"Answering service. Dr. Eliot isn't in his office on Saturday evenings."

Cat didn't like the woman's deprecating tone. "I assumed that," Cat said with an equally snide retort. "I'm a friend of his. I misplaced his home phone number."

"We don't give out the doctor's home number. If you leave your name and where you can be reached, I'll give Dr. Eliot the message when he calls in."

"Never mind." Cat hung up the phone. She glanced at her wristwatch. It probably wasn't too late to get hold of Ben and tell him she had changed her mind. She deliberated for a few minutes, happy afterward that she had delayed.

The phone rang as she was about to pick up the receiver to call Ben.

Luke's conversaton with Max hadn't resolved matters. All it did was confirm that Cat could cause Luke to make a fool out of himself, even when she wasn't around. Now Max could join the fast-accumulating league of people who would see him that way. Luke knew he was being overly hard on himself; Max Hart wasn't the kind of person who would relegate Luke to jester status merely on the basis of a benign fascination with a beautiful woman.

Luke tried to comfort himself with the thought that once this whole movie crew vanished from town, he could pretend the experience hadn't happened. That's not the best advice, he admonished himself. Wasn't he always telling patients to face their feelings and work them through? Usually he practiced what he preached. Cat Roy had managed to create an emotional chaos within him that had been running rampant for the past twenty-four hours.

He looked out his kitchen window, wondering when Cat's image would stop reappearing on that ledge across the street. He laughed aloud, replaying the whole scene in his mind. Then his thoughts moved to today's meeting at lunch. Was it his imagination that her eyes shone with anticipation when she'd told him the name of her hotel? What interest could she have in him? Cat was probably intimately involved with that suavely handsome older man that she kept wrapping her arms around. Luke told himself again that this infatuation with a woman he really knew absolutely nothing about was ridiculous.

It wasn't altogether true. He knew some things—the sultry sound of her laughter, the way her eyes kept changing color, her natural wit and feisty independence, the quality of vulnerability that surfaced despite her efforts to conceal it. That combination of spirit and fragility coupled with her exotic beauty was the cause of Luke's inability to put Cat Roy out of his mind. Maybe she was a little kooky, as Teri had said, but to Luke, that was part of Cat's appeal.

He walked back into the living room, stalked over to his desk, and picked up a psychiatric journal. No matter how enticing Cat was, there was no way he could imagine a viable relationship with her. It was no more plausible than his teenage fantasies about Sophia Loren divorcing Carlo Ponti and living in sin with him.

Even at seventeen Luke had strong ideas about staying single. Not necessarily as a lifelong goal but certainly until he was well established and secure in his professional identity. Luke had had to struggle to get through college and medical school, working all kinds of odd jobs fit in at odd hours to cover the high cost of education. His father had died when Luke was a child, and his mother was busy supporting three younger children and couldn't possibly swing the tuition. It had taken him three extra years to get through college going part-time, then he had to get his medical degree and begin his professional pursuits. Two months ago he had made the final installment payment on his last school loan. Writing out that last check to Union Bank and Trust had felt like a major milestone, and it marked an important turning point.

He stretched out on the couch, propping one leg up to support the journal. When he finished the book he was writing, it would mark yet another turning point for him; one which hopefully would put him at the top level of his profession. The fantasy of success, one that was far less threatening than those about Cat, helped get him through the article by Mandell about communication as a sexual enhancer.

When he finished the article, he moved to his desk, reread it, this time taking careful, detailed notes on file cards. Checking his watch, he realized it was time to call in to his answering service for messages. Weekends were a popular time for emotional crises, and Luke made a point of calling in almost every hour. When there was a real emergency, the service would dial into his beeper, but Luke had gotten in the habit of double-checking on the chance something came through that he should follow up on.

"Nothing, Doctor." The same nasal voice Cat had heard answered him, this time tinged with respect. "Oh, wait a minute. Someone did call but didn't leave any message. Or any name."

"Oh. Male or female?"

"A woman. Actually, she said she was a friend of yours. She asked for your home number, Doctor, but of course I explained that was impossible. I offered to—"

"Thanks, Doris," he cut her off abruptly. "That was fine. Just fine. I'll call in next hour." He hesitated. "On second thought, I'm going out tonight. Why don't I call back later this evening. I'll have my beeper so you can call through in an emergency. Only emergencies, though. Okay, Doris?"

"Certainly, Dr. Eliot. Even physicians deserve a night off."

"You're right, Doris. And that's exactly what I plan to do—take the night off."

He ran a comb through his hair, changed out of his jersey-knit rugby shirt into a crisply laundered, blue buttondown shirt, threw on a navy blazer, and started for the door. He came to a stop, tapped his forehead, and rushed into the kitchen for Cat's Thermos. He slipped it under his arm and headed for the Ambassador Hotel.

Cat hesitated as she reached for the phone. It could be any of a number of people calling— someone from the crew looking for company on a Saturday night, her father, or Carl with some last-minute changes. She took a deep breath and reached for the receiver.

"Hi."

"Luke?"

"I'm in the lobby. I stopped by to return your Thermos. If you're busy I could leave it—"

"Room 701. If you don't mind delivering door to door."

In the movie business you learn to move fast. Still, Cat must have broken all records for quick changes. By the time Luke knocked on her door, she had slipped on her new red dress, brushed her teeth again, slipped on tiny pearl earrings, dabbed on blush and lipstick, and was fastening the ankle strap on her sandals.

It took Luke a couple of seconds to catch his breath. Cat had taken it away when she'd opened the door.

Not only did she look absolutely dazzling—a fiery beauty in red—but there was an added breathless quality about her that made her all the more stunning.

"You are going out," he said, his voice strained.

87

She twirled around in an enchanting pirouette. "Do you like it?"

Words weren't coming easy. He nodded.

"Thanks for the Thermos," she said, prying it out from under his arm. "What would I do without it?"

They both grinned. "A pretty lame excuse," Luke admitted.

"I'm glad you dug up some reason to come over," she said, her breathlessness no longer having anything to do with racing around to get ready. She stepped aside to let him in.

Luke shut the door behind him. Cat set the Thermos on the small Queen Anne desk near her bed.

"I haven't been able to get you out of my mind." Luke's voice pierced the awkward silence. "I tried," he confessed.

Cat turned around to face him. "I tried, too."

He moved toward her. Cat could tell he was unsure of himself and unsure of her. She smiled, meeting him halfway. When he was beside her, he returned her smile and slipped his arms around her waist. Cat was amazed at the rush of arousal she felt at his touch. Her lips parted as his mouth met hers. He kissed her lightly, then looked down into her eyes. The taffeta crinkled as his hands slid down her slender body. Cat put her arms around his neck, snuggling closer. The dress crinkled some more. This time there was no hesitation as their lips met, the tentativeness giving way to pure desire.

Cat sighed as his lips traveled to the sensitive curve between her neck and shoulder. He ran his long fingers through her black hair, whispering her name softly, seductively against her ear. Cat's body tingled; her legs were weak as she pressed more tightly against him. She felt more shivery sensations as his hands ran down her body again.

One more kiss, she told herself, and then I'll pull myself together. Luke must have read her mind, bending his head to her lips once more, kissing her deeply, a hungry desire rippling through him.

Cat kept her silent promise. Her face flushed with excitement, her eyes the color of the sky at dusk, she pressed her hands lightly against his chest. This new passion was moving too quickly. She was never reluctant to take risks, but she always meticulously calculated the odds. This time she knew the odds were not in her favor.

"I think we'd better get out of this room—quick." Luke twisted a wayward strand of her hair between his fingers.

Even that gesture aroused her. She nodded. "I think you're right. How about showing me the town?"

He helped her on with a black fox jacket that blended perfectly with the ebony color of her hair. He really didn't want to leave. But he knew they should. He smiled as she fastened the fur and slipped her fingers through her hair, freeing the dark, silky strands from beneath her collar.

Cat gave him a Cheshire grin.

"Sometimes you're more kitten than Cat," he whispered.

She slipped her hand in his, gently tugging him toward the door. "Where do psychiatrists go on their evenings off?"

They munched on cheese dogs (Cat's without the "dog") and sipped beer from large styrofoam cups as the boat made its swing under the Golden Gate Bridge. A foghorn sounded in the mist. Cat finished eating, setting her half-filled cup on the bench as she leaned against the railing. Luke tossed the remains of his meal in the trash and put his arms around Cat, his cheek pressed against hers. Her skin was cool and satin-smooth, and as the wind whipped her hair every which way, Luke reflected on her natural beauty.

"So this is where you hang out when you take a break." She grinned, turning toward him. Her lips brushed his jaw.

"Far from the madding crowd." He kissed her lightly, then turned her to him to kiss her again. Afterward, when she tilted her head back, he smoothed her silken hair, which was damp from the sea mist. He smiled.

"What are you thinking?" she asked him.

"About how you looked drenched."

"Like a drowned rat." She giggled.

"Like a goddess risen from the dark, mysterious ocean." He skimmed his fingers down the slit of her jacket, touching her warm skin. "Golden tan body and the darkest blue eyes I'd ever seen. You took my breath away." He grinned. "Watching you stand on that ledge getting ready to leap to your death didn't help my troubled breathing."

She laughed, reaching out her arms to encircle his neck. Her eyes grew serious as he met her gaze. "I'm not a goddess, Luke."

He touched her cheek.

"We know nothing about each other, you know." She started to drop her hands to her side, but he caught her wrists, holding her fast.

"I know all I need to know."

She kept her eyes on him. "This is a little crazy."

"As a friend of mine once said, there's nothing wrong with being a bit crazy. In fact, since yesterday, it's a feeling I'm adjusting to surprisingly well."

Another foghorn blasted as the boat pulled into the pier. Cat leaned way over the railing to watch it dock.

Luke grabbed her elbow. "Watch it. I like you wet, but I prefer you dry."

"Did you ever see the movie *Message from the Deep*?" she asked.

Luke shook his head.

"It wasn't one of the top ten last year, but I did do some fabulous stunts in it. One in particular— where I had to hang over the side of a sinking ship while a hideous sea creature set off huge tidal waves." She leaned back over. "Want me to give you a brief preview?" she teased.

"No," he said gruffly, the light mood of the evening taking a sharp detour. Luke preferred his fantasy without a reminder of reality. That was exactly how he saw this night—magical, romantic, utterly removed from his real world and Cat's madcap life.

By the time they'd walked from Pier 39's west marina to Ghirardelli Square, Luke had recaptured the fantasy. Cat caught hold of his hand, leading him toward the chocolate factory off the main plaza. Like two little kids they watched chocolate being made, and then Luke bought giant silver-wrapped bars to snack on as they wound their way around the terraces, browsing in the shops, peering in the restaurant windows, and watching the central fountain spew foamy sprays of water.

The dreary, overcast day had given way to a cool, starlit night.

"I love San Francisco," Cat said, stretching sinuously.

She's always feline, Luke thought with a smile.

"Paris and San Francisco are the two places I always leave my heart," she added. Now especially San Francisco, she added to herself.

Luke put his arm around her, his fingers sinking luxuriously into the fur. "Paris is a lovely place to visit. San Francisco is a lovely place to live."

"Good point. You're very smart."

"Thanks."

"And very perceptive," she said. "You look good, too, sick or healthy."

He smiled, then studied her thoughtfully.

"Are you analyzing me after all, Doc? Still wondering what makes me tick?"

"I'm beginning to figure that out."

"You sound—disappointed."

"No." He smiled wistfully. "Just resigned." He slipped his hand in hers. He had almost asked her when she was leaving the city, but at that moment he didn't really want to know. He hugged her against him, glad for this night.

They wandered back down to the pier, stopping to listen to some Dixieland jazz at Earthquake McGoon's. They both liked New Orleans blues, but neither of them could concentrate. A crowded, smoky room was the wrong setting for their mood. They had one drink and left after Luke checked in with his answering service.

"You probably have to get up early for filming. Shall we head back to your hotel?" Luke asked as they stepped outside.

"Even stunt women get a day off," Cat said. "But let's go back to the hotel, anyway. We could have a nightcap or some coffee."

Back at the Ambassador they walked by a small cocktail lounge near the elevator. Neither of them suggested going in for that nightcap.

At the door to her hotel room Cat handed Luke her key. He opened the door and followed her inside.

She turned to face him. "I don't want you to go."

He came toward her. "You couldn't get me out

of here"—he paused as he undid the clasp of her jacket and slid the fur off her shoulders—"even if you threatened to jump out of your window."

Her soft, sensuous laughter became muffled as his lips captured the sound.

CHAPTER SIX

"No stunts now," Luke whispered.

Cat smiled and shook her head. She moved with a liquid grace over to the window and pulled open the curtains. A bright San Francisco moon lit the room like a stage setting before dawn. Etched in the light, Cat returned to Luke.

"That's better," she murmured breathily against his ear. "I want to see you clearly."

He undid the ribbon-thin belt of her dress, then slid his hand around back, reaching for the zipper.

"Did I tell you that you look exquisite tonight?" He unzipped the dress, pushing it off one shoulder. Lowering his head, he pressed his lips briefly against the swell of her breast. "You looked mighty good yesterday, too, in that cowgirl getup." He slipped the dress off her other shoulder. It crinkled as it fell to the floor. His hands moved from her shoulders, grazing her slender arms.

"What about now?" she asked seductively as she moved back a step and undid the front clasp of her bra, letting the flimsy black lace slip off.

All that remained was a pair of matching bikini panties that Luke removed before he answered her.

"Now," he whispered, his eyes wandering slowly down her body, "you are at your most beautiful."

Cat reached out and stroked his cheek. He had already taken off his jacket and shirt. She helped him remove the rest of his clothes.

She moved into his arms, fitting perfectly against him. Everything was perfect about this night.

So why did she feel a sudden wave of sadness? Luke must have sensed the change in her mood because he cupped his hand under her chin, tilting her head up so that their eyes met. "Cat, what is it?" he asked.

She shook her head, attempting a smile that didn't quite make it.

He stroked her back. "Listen to me. All my life I've carefully analyzed and weighed every step I took. Each goal was laid out, planned down to the minute. I'm thirty-six years old, Cat. So far, everything has gone according to my careful plans. Then yesterday I saw you, and I haven't been able to think clearly since." He bent and touched her lips. It was a sweet, tender kiss. "I don't think I've ever wanted any woman with the crazy intensity I feel for you. In case you haven't guessed, I am not usually this impulsive." He grinned. "I don't go

96

around rescuing maidens and seducing them." He gently traced his hand over her breasts, feeling her taut nipples against his palms. "I want to seduce you. God, how I want to."

Cat pressed her body against him with a fierceness that took Luke's breath away. "This night is going to end." There was a catch in her throat. "I always used to like endings. It meant the excitement of starting something new, different. Now"— she kissed his neck, his chest, his lips—"we haven't even begun and I'm falling to pieces over it ending. I need help, Doc."

He lifted her up and carried her over to the kingsize bed, sitting down with her on his lap. He cradled her against him, stroking her hair. "We can grab the moment, Cat." He held her away from him as he spoke. "Or we can be sensible, rational . . ."

"Organized. Planning every step," she finished for him. "In case you haven't figured it out already, that isn't my style." She laughed softly as Luke brushed his lips against her throat. "I was raised on backlots of movie sets. Sometimes I'm not altogether certain where and when the fantasy ends and reality begins. So much is make-believe in my world."

He tumbled back on the bed with her, holding her tightly as she clung to him. "This may be fantasy," he murmured, "but it isn't make-believe. My feelings aren't make-believe. Neither are yours. And the fantasy—it's one we share together, one we can always keep, despite endings."

Her lips curved in a half-smile. "Maybe it's only in the movies that the two of us could come together. We're an odd match, Luke. The producer would most likely turn down the script, saying it's too improbable, far too unrealistic."

"I thought we were talking about fantasy, not realism," Luke insisted. "And in my fantasy, you aren't supposed to talk about plausibility." He placed his palm against the small of her back, arching her to him.

She moaned softly. "Let's not talk at all." Pulling him closer, she whispered in a low, throaty voice, "Didn't someone just call 'Action'?"

Luke grinned. "Definitely."

He rolled her over on her back, feasting on her with his eyes, his hands, his lips. He did not want to miss a spot, needing to make every inch of her his own. For tonight. That thought brought a flash of private sadness, but he shrugged it off with determination. Tonight is all there is, and for once he was going to grab the moment without hesitation.

Her slightest touch aroused him to distraction. She delighted in his husky moans of pleasure as she explored his hard, firm body. Letting her hair trail down his chest, she slid her lips down to his stomach. His rippling muscles quivered at the feel of her tongue against his flesh. She ran her hands up his thighs, trailing her fingernails lightly along his flesh.

He kissed her, his tongue slipping deep into the recesses of her mouth. His hands caressed her full breasts, his palms skimming back and forth across her hardened nipples.

She whispered his name over and over, her passion skyrocketing, her body melting with a longing that made her think she might go truly mad with wanting him.

They had been ready for each other from the first moment. Now their kisses, their embraces became more demanding, the struggle to hold back any longer growing almost painful. When at last he filled her with exquisite joy, she surrendered fully to the magical fantasy of their night.

Afterward she snuggled against him, watching his fingers trace light lines down her arm. She sighed. "If you include tonight in your research, Dr. Eliot, that book of yours has got to be a smash hit."

She lifted herself on an elbow, studying his smile. Bending lower, she kissed the upturned edges of his lips, then slid her tongue from one corner to the other.

Luke grabbed for her. She lost her balance, tumbling over him. "I can never do enough research. And I'm learning so much. We really need to do further study, don't you think?"

"For science, Doc—anytime." She kissed him hard on the lips, then swung up one long leg almost to his shoulder. "Did I ever tell you I was double-jointed?"

"There may be ways to sexual fulfillment that I never even guessed at." He grinned, stroking her inner thigh. She arched her back, moving her body toward him in a way that clearly further proved her point—and drove him wild with hungry lust.

Cat made love without restraint. She was also the most inventive, agile lover Luke had ever known. He had seen her as a kitten, and now she was pure tiger—strong, insistent, powerful in her desire to meet all of their wants and needs. He responded with the same openness, discovering the special places that made her gasp for breath, cry out in husky sighs. He loved watching the expression of pleasure on her face as he made love to her.

A while later, his arms still around her, she fell asleep. Luke looked down at her hair feathered across his chest. He lifted a strand and coiled it lightly around his finger. She stirred a little and he drew her nearer. Cat sighed contentedly, a kitten once again.

Luke closed his eyes but he couldn't sleep. His mind slowly drifted in and out of reality. A picture of Cat sailing in space kept coming into focus. He still could not fathom how she could do some of the stunts her profession required. He had silenced Teri when she'd said the stunts could be dangerous, but he couldn't silence his own thoughts. Why couldn't she have been . . . what? A regular, everyday person with a nine-to-five career? Someone who didn't crash up cars, hang from precipices, run out of burning houses?

He started going over movies he had seen, imagining Cat as one of the stunt people in some of the more horrific scenes. She probably had actually stunted in a few of them. He found himself thinking that he was glad he didn't go to movies more often. And he doubted now that he would ever choose to go see the disaster films that were so popular nowadays. The stunts for those movies had to be especially dangerous.

"Are you asleep?" Cat's voice broke through his thoughts.

He hugged her. "No."

"What are you doing?" She tilted her head up to see him, pushing her hair away from her eyes.

He lay still, looking at her. When he spoke, his voice was very low. "Do you ever get frightened?"

"Doesn't everyone?"

"I mean, when you start to do a stunt, do you ever think it's too dangerous, too risky? Do you get scared?"

"Luke," she said, sitting up, "most stunts look scary to an outsider, but to those of us in the business, much of what we do is very routine, uncomplicated—and no riskier than crossing a city street at rush hour. If you wait for the right signal and don't dawdle, there's no reason in the world you won't make it to the other side in good shape."

"Uhm hmm." He nodded doubtfully.

"Okay. Some stunts can be tricky and a little dangerous," she admitted.

"The ones you particularly like—right?"

"I thought tonight was fantasy. Outside this room we both move in our own directions, doing the things that make sense to us. I love what I do,

Luke. It's as much a part of me as—as breathing. There is nothing like the thrill and excitement of accomplishing a wild, daring feat. I could never live any other kind of life. Anything that even hints of routine makes me wilt. You don't want me to shrivel up, do you?" She pursed her lips in a teasing grimace.

"Never." He smiled, believing what she said was true, and knowing, as he held her against him, that all he could ever capture of her was this night of fantasy.

"Are you hungry?" she asked.

"Interested in more research?"

"No, food. Though afterward I might have some more energy for scientific pursuits."

He laughed, reaching over to the nightstand for his watch. The moonlit room provided enough light for him to see that it was three o'clock in the morning.

"It's kind of early for breakfast."

"Let's call room service," she suggested. "It's available twenty-four hours."

Cat wanted chocolate cake and champagne. Luke opted for the champagne.

"Tell them to put a scoop of ice cream on the side—pistachio, if they have it."

When he hung up the phone, he told her she would have to settle for plain vanilla. That was all they had.

"How dull." She sighed

"You even demand excitement in your ice cream?" he teased.

"In everything," she said seriously. "Tonight fits that need of mine exquisitely."

He kissed her, drawing her to him. She reached her arms around his neck and kissed him back. She forgot about her ice cream and everything else as they started to make love again.

There was a light rap on the door a few minutes later. Cat groaned and started to lift herself off Luke. He pulled her back down.

"My ice cream is going to melt." She laughed as she struggled out of his grasp. Grabbing hold of the top sheet, she slipped off the bed.

"Hey! You can't leave me here naked like this."

She'd wrapped the sheet around her body, leaving him fully exposed on the bed. She giggled, looking back over her shoulder as she reached for the doorknob. "You look good to me."

He rolled across the bed onto the floor as Cat opened the door to the bellhop.

"Just wheel it inside for me," she said casually. "Oh, darling," she called in Luke's direction, "do you have any change on you?"

He mumbled something incoherent from his hiding place. Cat grinned. "That's okay. I've got some money in my purse."

The bellhop shifted awkwardly from one foot to the other. What the hell was that guy doing under the bed? "Do you want me to—uh—open the champagne for you?" he asked timidly, stifling a yawn. He had been hoping to get some shut-eye down in the kitchen. Not too many people wanted chocolate cake and champagne at three in the morning.

"Darling," Cat called again in that lilting falsetto, "should the boy open the bottle?"

"No!" he yelled.

"No thanks, then," she said cheerily, walking over to where Luke was squatting down beside the bed, hiding from the bellhop's view. "Just getting my purse, dear," she explained, reaching across his back. When she straightened up, she pinched his buttock, making him jump in surprise. She giggled. "Did you find that shoe yet?"

Cat tipped the bellhop generously and showed him out. She looked back at the bed, waiting for Luke to get up. There was no movement.

"Did you see the look on that boy's face? No, I guess you didn't." She took a few steps toward the bed. "Are you mad?" No answer. "It was only a joke." She moved to Luke's side of the bed. He was sitting on the floor, leaning against the mattress, legs outstretched, arms stolidly crossed at his chest.

"You are crazy."

She tilted her head slightly with a contrite expression on her face.

"Come over here."

She hesitated. "My ice cream is melting."

"You don't like vanilla, anyway. Come here."

She walked over to him. When she was within reach, he grabbed for her leg. She fell down half on top of him, the draped sheet around her coming undone.

"I am going to have to do something about these

104

audacious impulses of yours, young woman," he scolded lightly. "This is the second time you've put me in a very embarrassing situation."

"He didn't even see you," she countered, putting her fingers through his unruly hair.

"Mighty good thing he didn't." He reached under her knees and brought her fully onto his lap. "That bellhop happens to be the patient I saw in my office at seven o'clock this morning."

"Oh, Luke," she said, and broke out into a peal of giggling.

"It isn't all *that* funny," he said, feigning consternation. He couldn't suppress a broad grin. "Talk about compromising positions. Can you imagine that poor kid's reaction if he saw his psychiatrist hiding stark-naked under a hotel bed?"

They fell against each other laughing. When the laughter died down, Luke's expression became thoughtful.

"I'm sorry I put you in that position." She tried to apologize with a straight face, but her double entendre pleased her too much. She ended up laughing again.

He had to smile. But the episode with the bellhop brought home the reality that, as a psychiatrist, he had to uphold a certain image. Cat had no such restraints.

"Unfortunately, I'm not free to let loose and do something zany in public. I've bumped into patients in all kinds of places. It's always a little awkward. None as awkward as this time—even if you had left me that sheet." His lips curved into a slight smile.

Cat cursed herself for spoiling the romantic mood. Sometimes she was too impulsive for her own good.

"Go ahead and eat your ice cream," he said, his hand covering his mouth as he yawned.

"I'm not hungry anymore," she said, getting up. "Let's get back into bed."

She got up, pulling the sheet with her and spreading it back on the bed. She slipped underneath. Luke walked over to the table, opened the bottle, and poured them both some champagne. Cat took a glass from his outstretched hand. He joined her under the sheet, glass in hand.

"What do we toast to?" Cat asked softly.

"To our moonlit night filled with fantasy and excitement at the Ambassador Hotel."

They clinked glasses and drank the champagne down.

Luke pressed Cat's head to his chest and put his arms around her. Within minutes, her breathing was deep and even, and when he shut his eyes this time, he, too, fell asleep.

They were rudely awakened in the late morning by the shrill ring of the phone. Cat groaned, still warmly nestled in Luke's light embrace.

"Who is it?"

Luke stretched. "I think you have to pick up the receiver to find out."

"Oh." She reached out, her eyes still closed, fumbling around on the table until her hand closed around the phone. As she lifted the receiver, the bottom half of the phone fell with a thud to the floor. She turned away from Luke and bent over to retrieve it.

Luke's hand stroked her back as she leaned half off the bed. Then, grinning, he pinched her bottom, sending her tumbling off the bed. She let out a little shriek as she fell.

"Hello." She climbed back onto the bed, phone in hand, scowling at Luke.

"Everything okay, Cat?"

"Oh, Dodger. Sure. Yeah. Fine." The words, stilted and staccato, made their way out of her mouth.

"Do you want to go over tomorrow's crash? I have a few ideas I think might add a new angle or two."

"Today?"

"Of course today. When else? You didn't mention any plans. And you know I like to make sure you are razor-sharp about the procedure."

"Dodger, give me a break, will you? I know the game plan like the back of my hand. If you have a couple of changes we can go over them tomorrow morning. I'm not scheduled till three in the afternoon."

"Do me a favor and don't show off tomorrow."

"What the hell is that supposed to mean?"

"Watch your language, little girl." His Mississippi drawl, still with him from childhood despite all his years in Hollywood, came back full force. It always did when he scolded her. "You took that

107

leap too wide yesterday. And you were too tense. That's why you nearly broke your wrist."

"It was barely a sprain," she argued, her own inflection growing more southern. "I took the dumb bandage off right after you walked away yesterday."

"That's just what I mean—showing off."

"Dodger." She grimaced at the receiver and then across to Luke, shaking her head.

"You are stubborn as the day is long, Cat. But you always were, so I don't know why I still let myself get all riled up about it. I'll speak to you later."

"Have a nice day, Dodger," she said sweetly, and hung up.

"Gave you a tough time, huh?"

"Always does, always will," she said, stepping out of bed. "But then, he's the boss."

"Is he the one that dishes out the rewards, too?" The phone call had produced a decidedly sour taste in Luke's mouth, and a definite dose of reality to his mind.

"What are you talking about?" She gave him a puzzled look.

"I'm talking about a six-foot-plus man in his early fifties with a magnificent athlete's body and a craggy face that has probably crushed dozens of hearts across the continent."

Cat laughed. "Dodger would love that description. You're right on target, Doc."

"Your heart's still intact, though," he observed.

"Dodger and I go way back. We're—we're a family." Her eyes, a crisp, clear blue in the daylight sun, sparkled mischievously. "We're always hugging and kissing—when we aren't fighting."

"How Hollywood."

"Luke, you are funny."

"There's nothing funny about loose morals."

"Oh, so that's what Hollywood people are like. Wanton women, heartbreaking men, orgies, drugs . . ."

"Is that so off the track?"

"Not for some, I guess. But I don't particularly care for that brand of fulfillment. Dodger and I are—"

"That's all right," he stopped her abruptly. "It isn't any of my business. What you and Dodger do—what you and any man do in your life—does not require explanations."

"Well, thank you, Dr. Eliot." She said tersely. Then she lay back on the pillow. "This is no way to wake up to the man you've just spent the best night of your life with."

Luke grabbed a hold of Cat's hand, bringing it to his lips. He kissed the tip of each finger.

She stuck one of her fingers into his mouth, then rolled over toward him, transferring the same finger to her own mouth for a moment.

Luke grinned. "You are sinfully, deliciously wanton, tiger." He slid his hand under her hip, firmly grabbing her to draw her more tightly to him.

She nuzzled her lips into the crook of his neck, then whispered in his ear, "With you I'm very

Hollywood. Let's have another private orgy. What do you say?"

"I say it's the best idea you've had all morning." He kissed her hard on the lips for emphasis.

They made love again. But it wasn't the same as last night. The passion was there; the hunger, the ecstasy was recreated. And yet, there was a sense of urgency, of time running out that they both silently felt, fought against acknowledging and, in the end, secretly admitted.

The night had cast an aura of timelessness around them, nestling them in a safe cocoon while they learned about each other and made love basking in the soft glow of the moon. But now the sun cast a harsher, stronger light. Reality had entered Cat's room at the Ambassador Hotel, and they both knew it. Still, they held on to the moment a little while longer.

Cat buried her head in his chest, tracing circles around his biceps. She had thought him strikingly sensual when he tried to talk her off the ledge and then again as he hugged his robe around his torso while she forced her brew on him in his apartment. But last night and today she had discovered the true depths of his sensuality. Luke Eliot could easily become an addiction. And she did still have another eight days in town. . . .

Luke ran his fingers through her wild, thick, tangled hair, lifting it away from her face. His touch was tender, loving. He hugged her tightly for a minute, then relaxed his grip.

She found herself thinking about Teri Caul-

110

field—Dr. Caulfield, as the cool, sophisticated blond had so pointedly corrected. Doctor and doctor. Now that was a match made in heaven. Any producer would buy that romance. Even the contrasts—her fairness against his dark good looks; her slight, small, willowy frame beside his tall, broad torso—were not antithetical. The differences between them were just enough to add a spark of interest.

Cat and Luke were a great physical match, but they were diametrically opposed in spirit, personality, style. . . . She vetoed the eight days she might be able to wangle with Luke. What was the point? Why would she want to torment herself by getting even more deeply involved with a man when the ending was so obvious? No one would bother to see their film—if someone was fool enough to make it.

She lifted her head up and gazed at Luke. He traced the contours of her face with his index finger. When it passed her lips, she bit his finger lightly and smiled. Just as she bent to kiss him the phone rang again.

She was brief and a little surly as she told the caller that she was still sleeping and to call back later.

Luke watched her hang up the phone.

"Dodger again?"

"No."

"Another member of the family?"

"You mean like a kissin' cousin?" Cat teased.

"Do you know that before I met you, I would

111

have sworn on a stack of bibles that I did not have a jealous bone in my body."

"Come on, Doc. You trying to tell me the beautiful Dr. Caulfield never caused those bones to poke out?" She bit her lip, angry with herself. She had been determined not to bring up Teri Caulfield. Luke was right. What went on in their real lives had no bearing on their private fantasy.

"Teri?" There was questioning surprise in his tone. Then, slapping his palm against his forehead, just like they always do in movies when the light dawns, he sprang out of bed, gaped at his watch and exclaimed, "Teri!"

Now it was Cat's turn to look surprised. "What is it?"

"I don't believe it. It's ten minutes after twelve. I was supposed to be there by now." He was dashing around the room, retrieving the clothes that he had so casually tossed aside last night. He hopped up and down on one foot as he slipped on his sock, then switched feet to put on the other. He continued hopping into his underwear and trousers, then wriggled into his loafers. "I'm not even going to have time to stop back at my apartment to shower and change. I'll have to grab a cab and—no, wait, maybe she hasn't left her apartment yet. Jeez. Matheson went on at noon. I'm going to miss most of his presentation."

Cat got out of bed, walked over to her closet, and put on a robe. "When you take your next breath, would you fill me in?"

He stopped dead in his tracks, shirt half-buttoned.

112

"I'm supposed to meet Teri at the Drake for a very important medical conference. Matheson—he's the speaker I'm missing now—is one of the key contributors to my book. If nothing else, it does not look very good for me to be absent at his presentation. I also happen to be extremely interested in hearing it. At least I'll get there before he finishes—if I hurry."

"By all means, hurry up." She turned away, angry at the catch in her throat. A moment later she felt his hands on her shoulders.

"Not a great ending. Turn around."

"You'll miss Matheson."

"Sometimes my priorities get a little out of whack." He turned her around. "You want to hear a piece of self-analysis?"

"What?"

"I think I was starting to feel like it would be too hard to say good-bye—too painful. So I was going to fly out of here to avoid the feeling. It wouldn't have worked. The pain would follow me out the door. In fact, I have a feeling it's going to follow me around for quite a while."

"Mind if we share that analysis?" She blinked a tear away and draped her arms around his neck. They kissed good-bye.

Luke walked out her door, Cat climbed back into bed, moving over to his still-warm side. That kiss was meant to be good-bye. It was the smartest, most rational thing to do. They had grabbed the moment and now had to set it free. So why did she feel like that kiss hadn't tasted of farewell?

113

Luke rode down in the elevator, rubbing a finger against his lips. He had a funny feeling that had not been the last farewell kiss he and Cat would share. He argued with himself all the way to The Drake that his feeling was ridiculous. He and Cat both knew there was no point in seeing each other again. This good-bye had been hard enough.

CHAPTER SEVEN

Ben called Cat back half an hour after Luke left. In that half an hour she had showered, dressed, and sulked. When she picked up the phone on its fourth ring, her voice was lower, huskier than usual.

"Still asleep?"

"No."

"Have any plans for today?"

"No."

"Are you feeling okay?"

"No."

"Are you sick?"

"No."

"Do you want to talk about it? Skip it. I can guess the answer."

"What are you doing today?" Cat asked impulsively, throwing Ben off kilter. He was sure she had been about to hang up on him.

"I'm open to anything—if you'll come along."

"I don't think I'm going to be a lot of fun."

"I'll take my chances. It's the first sunny day we've had since we hit this town. That alone should perk up your spirits, no matter what I come up with."

"I don't know, Ben. Dodger called before. He wanted me to go over some new angles on the crash tomorrow."

"Forget Dodger. I just saw him leave the hotel with Joanie."

"Joanie Weston? Oh, he probably wants to check on some effects."

"I'm sure he does." Ben chuckled

"Ben, don't be disgusting."

"Come on, Cat. Dodger is a man as well as your father. A mighty good-looking guy at that. Joanie isn't all that bad, either."

"She's almost half his age." She paused. "Isn't she?"

"Since when does age have anything to do with love?"

"The only thing Dodger loves is a well-executed stunt—besides me."

"Hey, you really are bugged by the idea of Dodger and Joanie getting it—"

"Drop it, Ben. I'm not bugged. It just feels a little weird, that's all. Dodger's certainly had plenty of women in his life, but he usually keeps his private life separate from work. It's just a little awkward. Joanie and I have become real friendly on this picture."

"So, what's the problem? She'll make a great stepmom."

"Oh, stop it, Ben. Are you pulling my leg about all this? How do you know they didn't go off to do some work?"

"Okay, okay. If it will make you feel any better, that's probably what they did. I must have mis-read the signals."

"What signals?" she asked, then decided not to pursue it. "Forget it. I'll meet you down in the lobby in ten minutes. Put your mind to work on *our* plans for the day, instead of Dodger's."

"Good. Let's both put everyone else out of our minds and concentrate on each other today."

He hung up before Cat could question his last remark. Did he know that Luke had spent the night in her room? No, she decided, how could he know?

When Ben hung up the phone in the lobby, he went to the Ambassador book stand. As he thumbed through a San Francisco tour guide, quickly scan-ning it for ideas, he thought about Cat. He'd been to the city plenty of times, but today he wanted to find something special, something that would make Cat forget that doctor who had just spent the night with her. He'd seen Luke Eliot racing through the lobby about thirty minutes ago. The doctor looked like a man who needed a shave and a change of clothes.

Luke rubbed the side of his cheek. He really did need to shave before he showed up at that conference. And brush his teeth. Passing a mirror at the Drake, he was shocked at the grubby state of his appearance and ended up buying a disposable razor from the gift shop. In the men's room, he did his best to work up a later with the liquid soap from the metal dispenser and scrape off the surface of his stubble. Then he gargled with some tap water, combed his hair with his fingertips, and went to face his colleagues. He felt decidedly disoriented.

Todd Archer had taken Luke's seat beside Teri. She hadn't even held another one for him. When Luke caught her eye, she gave him an icy nod of greeting and turned to Archer, whispering something in his ear.

Luke found a seat next to Max Hart just as Tom Matheson was accepting questions from the distinguished audience.

"How did it go?" Luke asked in a low voice.

"According to Matheson, don't swallow a handful of tranquilizers if you're trying to make time with your lady love."

Luke smiled uncomfortably, feeling even more disoriented as Max took in his appearance and grinned broadly.

"Where did you just come from? A night on a park bench?"

"Do I look that awful?" Luke asked.

Max chuckled. "For anyone else, no. For you—a man who has always dared wrinkles and smudges to even try to touch him—you look terrible."

Luke ran his fingers through his hair.

Max patted Luke's knee. "Don't worry about it. The world is not going to collapse because Luke Eliot didn't change his suit today."

"I'm not thinking about the world."

A large balding man with a beard sitting behind Luke asked him to be quiet. Luke apologized and tried to pay attention to the rest of the questions. He spotted Teri looking over her shoulder at him. This time her glance was less frigid. Luke smiled, beginning to feel like things were returning to some semblance of normality.

The lobby of the Ambassador was bustling with activity. A large busload of people had just arrived for a three-day dental technicians' convention. Ben was standing near the check-in counter, doing some careful checking of his own. Some of the dental technicians were very young and very attractive. More than a couple of them noticed the same was true of Ben Seaton.

As Cat walked over, Ben dropped his survey and gave her all his attention, but not before he took a quick glance in a nearby mirror to make sure he was looking good.

Cat noticed his action, a flash of annoyance at Ben's vanity surfacing. Even his casual pose looked artificial and contrived.

She reminded herself of her vow to keep her spirits up. By the time she stood beside Ben, she managed a warm, friendly smile. "Did you come up with any ideas?"

Ben grinned seductively, but Cat's scowl quickly

sobered him. "How about lunch aboard one of the tour boats?"

"No." She hadn't meant to sound so angry. Smiling apologetically, she added, more softly, "I tend to get seasick."

"Oh." Ben thought fast for an alternative idea. Cat was wearing an expression he correctly interpreted as rapidly losing interest in any plan.

He took her hand. "Let me surprise you. I promise no boat rides."

"And I don't want chocolate from Ghirardelli Square, either," she had to tell him. If she was going to spend this day getting Luke Eliot off her mind, then she couldn't have Ben unwittingly replay the fantasy. She shot him a sideways glance. Besides, she admitted wistfully, Ben wasn't the right star for the role.

They had a pleasant lunch in Chinatown. Cat tried to maintain her interest as Ben did the talking—mostly about himself. Whenever the stunning Eurasian waitress passed their table, he flashed her his most winning smile. Cat had no doubt that if she excused herself to go to the ladies' room, Ben would surely have made a date with the waitress by the time she returned.

She didn't care. For one thing, she never could muster up any romantic interest in Ben. He was like so many of the men in the business—freewheeling and egotistical. At least Ben had some charm and was basically good-natured. It softened the self-centeredness enough for Cat to like him. If she wasn't feeling so low, she would probably be enjoying herself right now. Ben was certainly trying his best.

"Have you decided about the Logan film yet? Dave Norman is doing the special effects and asked if I wanted to do some work on it. He mentioned that he asked you, too."

Cat took a fortune cookie from the plate the waitress had brought over with the bill.

"Let's see what Confucius thinks." Cat smiled. The smile faded as she read the slip of paper. She tossed it on the table.

Ben picked it up and read out loud. " 'Love is like a rose—prickly thorns and sweetly scented petals.' " He looked across at Cat. "Something tells me we should avoid the Botanical Gardens this afternoon."

Cat's smile returned. "How about renting a car and taking a drive to Muir Woods? We can climb Mt. Tamalpais."

A long, exhausting hike up a mountain hadn't been exactly part of Ben's plan, but the idea seemed to perk up Cat's spirits, and that was foremost on his mind. Once they were on top of the mountain, she might have burned off enough nervous energy to be more receptive to other ideas.

They stopped back at the hotel where Cat, already in blue jeans and cowboy shirt, changed out of her sandals into a comfortable pair of sneakers. She had climbed Mt. Tamalpais a couple of years ago with Dodger when they were out here filming *Playing It Safe*.

She knew Mt. Tamalpais was not a particularly

difficult hike, but climbing 2,600 feet toward the sky had to be tiring. Even though last night had provided little sleep, she was too keyed-up to be exhausted. A good climb in the fresh, cool air might calm her down. And it would keep Ben busy for a while. She was well aware that he was angling for an opportunity to make his moves. For a fleeting moment she considered the possibility of allowing him to succeed. It was one way to forget about last night.

Cat insisted on sharing the cost of the car rental. Stunt people earned respectable livings—when they had work—but they were far from rich.

The drive to Muir Woods took less than half an hour, especially as Ben was heavy-footed on the accelerator pedal. Car and cycle trick work was Ben's specialty. He could throw a motorbike at fifty miles an hour and walk away, as though he'd just stepped off a trolley car. He was a well-liked stunter, but Cat felt that Ben's need to show off created too many close calls. He and Dodger often locked horns working together on films. For all Dodger's daring and expertise, he put in as much time going through exacting calculations of the odds as he did doing stunts. Ben was a lot more casual and overly confident.

"Ben, take it easy tomorrow morning when you do that chase gag."

"You sound like Dodger. But from you, it's comforting. So you do care a little?" Ben put his arm around her shoulder as they started down a nature trail carpeted in pine needles.

"Don't push it," she warned. "I don't like being crowded." To emphasize her point she lifted Ben's arm away. Craning her neck up, she stared at the huge redwoods. "Did you ever see anything more beautiful?" She gave Ben a wide grin. "And don't you dare say me. I'm immune to old lines."

"Will I make any headway if I come up with some new ones? If the answer is yes, I'll do my damnedest to put my imagination to work."

"Ben, you're a sweet guy. . . ."

"I know. You want to be friends. What does that stuffy, uptight doctor have that I don't?"

Cat didn't answer.

"Hey, listen, if we're going to be friends, maybe it would help to talk about it. You've really fallen for this dude, haven't you?"

"Don't call him a dude!" she snapped. There was no one in the world more unlike a dude than Luke Eliot. "And I haven't fallen for him. This isn't the movies. In real life you don't fall in love with someone at first sight. That's crazy."

Crazy. That was a word that had come up in Cat's vocabulary in the last three days more than it had the rest of her life. Everything about her relationship with Luke was crazy.

"Maybe not love," Ben continued, in spite of Cat's flare-up, "but people can experience an immediate attraction for one another that can pack quite a wallop. Believe me, I know."

Cat turned to Ben. She kissed him on the cheek. "I'm sorry, Ben. You're right. People can feel . . .

123

something strong from that first moment. Unfortunately, those kinds of feelings don't always mesh with reality." She paused briefly. "Believe me, I know."

Ben took her hand. "Let's go climb a mountain."

The conference broke at three for coffee and doughnuts. Luke was just biting into a sugary cruller, his first taste of food that day, when Teri tapped him on the shoulder.

"Oh, Teri. Hi. I—uh . . ." He swallowed the bite of doughnut whole, coughing as he covered his mouth to prevent the crumbs from escaping.

Teri took a step away. "You must have gotten your cold back. You certainly don't look well, Luke."

"Yes—well, um, that's why I was late. I had a restless night."

"Really. That's too bad." She paused to select a glazed doughnut, taking a demure bite. "You must have been sleeping soundly around seven this morning. I called you several times. No answer." Her smile was tight, accentuating the tiny creases at the sides of her mouth.

He could have told her about Cat. It was certainly not like he'd cheated on Teri. They did not have that kind of relationship. And he certainly had nothing to be embarrassed about. He was a healthy red-blooded male who had a natural attraction to a gorgeous, sensuous, blue-eyed female. On the other hand, he didn't owe Teri any explanations.

The most important reason he kept silent was because he did not want to ruin the fantasy. Standing in the middle of a medical conference with all of his colleagues and friends, Luke could almost believe that Cat really was an exquisite figment of his imagination. Maybe it was better that way. He made a silent promise to get himself back on an even keel.

He started by apologizing to Teri.

"Forget it, Luke. I don't know why I've been so touchy lately. Must be the strain of the extra hospital work I've taken on." She smiled brightly and asked Luke if he wanted to join her for the rest of the conference.

Todd Archer looked a bit out of joint when he moved over to give Luke a seat next to Teri. Luke wondered if Archer was more interested in Teri than he'd assumed. He found himself wishing he could feel a spark of jealousy at the thought, but like he'd told Cat, that was a feeling only she seemed to be able to provoke. It hadn't taken him long—only a couple of minutes—for his mind to drift back to Cat.

Straightening in his seat, he focused all the attention he could muster on the rest of the speakers. Every so often a fleeting thought of Cat would crop up, set off by an odd word or expression, but he quickly doused the image, reminding himself how adept he was, when having to listen attentively to patients all day, at blocking out his own personal thoughts. But this afternoon was a real challenge to his skill.

At five o'clock the last paper was presented. It had been the one on over-the-counter medications that Teri had been so interested in hearing. Todd Archer, an internist like Teri, chatted away with her after the question-and-answer period. Luke was feeling bored and was looking around for Max when Teri turned her attentions to him.

"Terrific presentation, don't you think?"

"Yes. Yes. It was excellent."

Harvey Rothman, a psychiatrist who had gone to medical school with Luke, edged his way over to the threesome. After shaking hands with Archer and greeting Teri with an affectionate pat on the back, he began talking with Luke about the conference.

"I saw you walk in at the end of Matheson's paper. Too bad. He made some interesting points about the dynamics underlying the need for tranquilizers as an unconscious ploy to avoid sexual involvement."

Teri leaned closer. "Sneakier than the old headache ploy."

Todd Archer laughed the loudest. Luke spotted Max and waved him over. Tonight he wasn't up for long-winded analytical conversations and deep psychological diatribes. He could always count on Max to provide some needed levity. Max had spent years encouraging Luke not to be so intense. He had succeeded at least in teaching Luke not to take himself too seriously. Unlike many of his erudite colleagues, when Luke behaved pompously, he was aware of it. His natural, relaxed, unaffected style was actually what made him so popular among those in his profession.

Max put his arm around Luke as he joined the group.

"I don't know about the rest of you, but all that talking and having to think made me thirsty. How about you?" He addressed them all but looked at Luke.

"They're just setting up for the cocktail party, Max. Why not wait a little while?" Teri suggested, still wanting to discuss some points with Todd. On the other hand, she was determined not to let Luke slip through her fingers tonight.

Teri knew damn well he had lied to her about sleeping too soundly to hear the phone this morning. For some reason, the idea that he had been off on some kind of liaison encouraged this new budding interest in Luke as a potential lover.

She had been working too hard lately, she'd concluded the third time she'd tried Luke's number that morning. And the end result had been a lot of lonely nights in bed these past couple of years. Since her luncheon date yesterday with Luke, she'd decided that she wanted to make some definite changes in their relationship.

Luke agreed with Max that it would be pleasant to go off to the bar across the street as a break from all the intellectual stimulation around them. Teri reluctantly nodded agreement. Actually, she loved the quality of excitement a good conference generated. And this had been a particularly stimulating one. She cast Luke a curious glance. He really was going through some changes. Usually he seemed as enthusiastic as she was to share thoughts and current happenings with colleagues at these conferences. And once they sat down to the formal dinner that invariably concluded these conferences, they would have little chance to talk with anyone but the people at their table.

But tonight she thought it was important enough to forego the intellectual pleasures for some more emotional ones. She'd do what Luke wanted. She slipped her hand in his, weaving her fingers through his, as she Luke, and Max crossed the street.

The sunlit day had given way to a cool, windy evening, and a misty drizzle started. By the time they stepped into the small bar, the three of them felt chilled. Teri excused herself to fix her wind-blown hair in the ladies' room while Max and Luke slid into a small booth, bending their heads so as not to crash into the low-hung, ornate Tiffany-style lamp.

The waitress came over and Max ordered a double martini. Luke told her to make that two, and ordered a Scotch for Teri. He stared down at the table, seeing a vision of Cat, hair flying in the ocean breeze, sipping her beer from a styrofoam cup. He flushed slightly as he became aware that the image alone had aroused him.

Max was silent. In his profession, comfortable silences were a necessary skill. Luke looked across at him.

"I need a vacation, Max."

"I agree, my friend."

Luke laughed nervously. "That patient of mine—the one I told you about yesterday . . ." His lips curved in a sheepish grin.

"Ah, the man with the burning infatuation for a tempestuous spirit. Yes, I remember that discussion."

"Max, you're a subtle devil. No wonder you're such a successful psychiatrist."

"So, you want to give me some follow-up?"

"That was no park bench I slept on last night." Luke smiled wanly.

"The question is—where will you sleep tonight?" Max removed the two olives from his drink, set them in the ashtray, and took a hefty swallow of his martini.

Luke sighed. "In three weeks I'm off to sunny Greece. I need complications in my life right now like I need bubonic plague. The definitive answer to your question, Max, is that tonight and every night for the next three weeks I am sleeping at home—and alone."

Max nodded slightly in the direction to the left of Luke's shoulder. "I think your Dr. Caulfield has some other ideas about your residency."

As if on cue, Teri swept into the bench seat beside Luke and said, "I have a great idea."

Luke shot an amused glance at Max and then looked sideways at Teri.

Her blond hair, usually neatly pinned back in a

bun, was now billowing loosely in shimmering softness around her shoulders. The even more striking change was the look of purpose and determination in her jade-green eyes.

Luke marveled at Max's insightful mind, but then wondered if maybe he wasn't being unusually dense these past few days. All the wires in his brain seemed to have come detached and reconnected with the wrong circuitry.

"Well, do you want to hear it?"

Luke nodded. Max didn't move a muscle but he knew Teri was only interested in Luke's response.

"Instead of going back to the dinner at the Drake, how about picking up some steaks and salad fixings and going back to my apartment for a quiet, relaxed evening?" Her glance invited both of them, but she was pretty confident Max would get the message and beg off.

"No, not tonight, Teri. But thanks."

"I just thought—you looked so tired and you've been so sick these past few days. . . ." Her voice was tinged with disappointment, but she had too much class to take her arguments any further. Teri Caulfield did not beg. "Another time."

"Yeah. Good idea. It's just that I should talk with Matheson tonight, and there were a few other people I need to touch base with."

Max had remained quiet during the discussion. Now, as Teri lifted her Scotch, he picked up his half-finished martini and tapped her glass. "Here's to you, Teri. You look especially lovely tonight."

A warm flush colored her cheeks as she smiled at Max. Luke smiled at him, too. He could always count on him to save the day.

Later that night, after a lukewarm dinner of dried-out chicken, pasty rice, and a nondescript salad at the conference, Luke took Teri home by taxi. She didn't ask him up for a nightcap because she perceived that Luke would probably turn her down. But she did lean over toward him, and instead of the perfunctory peck on the lips that marked their traditional good-bye, she kissed him full on the mouth, her tongue lightly skimming his own sealed lips.

Teri smiled, privately pleased with herself. Luke may not have been very responsive, but there was a definite glint in his eye as they said good night. Given time, she had complete confidence he'd be the one suggesting the nightcaps.

Luke had the taxi continue on to his apartment. He leaned back against the backseat, exhausted and totally perplexed. For months he had been so immersed in work, he'd had no time for any intimate involvements, even brief interludes. And now, in one short weekend he had seduced one woman and been seduced by another. Almost seduced, that is. Luke would have had to be a eunuch not to have felt any response to Teri's sensual kiss, but deep down, what it stirred the most was yet a fiercer desire for Cat.

Cat. Kitten. Tiger. Luke sighed, forcing himself to conjure up visions of Mediterranean breezes and salty sea air. His sabbatical could not come quickly enough. If ever there was a place to forget tempestuous spirits, he was banking on it being Greece.

CHAPTER EIGHT

On Monday morning, Cat met Dodger downstairs in the lobby of their hotel. She was dressed in her traditional jeans but had chosen a cotton-knit sweater done in soft pastel blue, green, and pink stripes instead of her usual cowboy shirt. The selection had been a deliberate attempt to perk up her appearance and add some color to her complexion.

She should have known better than to think she could hide anything from Dodger. The biggest giveaway was her makeup. Cat rarely bothered with that stuff unless she had something to hide.

"What happened to your face?"

"No good morning? Would you like some breakfast?" Cat asked, making a concerted effort to keep her tone light and easy. She knew if Dodger thought she was too wiped out he'd never let her go ahead with her stunt this afternoon.

"You look like hell, little girl," Dodger said, ignoring her efforts to get him off the subject. His drawl was strong, and Cat knew there was no point sidestepping the issue.

"I didn't get that much sleep last night, but"—she hastily went on to add—"I plan to take a nice long nap before work. I'm not due till two."

"Yeah, well," he mumbled, grabbing her arm and steering her toward the coffee shop, "you haven't taken a nap since you were a baby. We'll just have to see."

A waitress tugged her order pad out of the lace-trimmed apron she wore around her ample middle. "What'll it be, folks?"

"Coffee for me," Cat said.

"Since when do you drink coffee? What about all those speeches about how caffeine—"

"Dodger, I don't think the waitress wants to wait around for a lecture about the evils of caffeine." She looked back up at the woman and smiled. "Make that two coffees, and I guess I'll have"—she bit her bottom lip studying the menu—"an English muffin with that."

"She'll have a couple of eggs over easy, too. Same for me. And a rasher of bacon. In fact, throw in a side order of sausage. Do the eggs come with home fries?"

The waitress, still busy scribbling down the order, nodded.

"Good. Bring over the coffee now, doll." Dodger

gave her a seductive wink, which Cat was sure would definitely make the woman's day—maybe her week. Dodger was a man who knew how to get good service.

"You'd better watch that boyish figure of yours, Dodger. Younger women like their older men in good physical shape." Cat smiled broadly, but there was an underlying sarcasm to her words that Dodger did not miss.

"And what is that remark supposed to mean?" Dodger asked with a scowl.

"No hidden meaning," Cat insisted, concentrating on the coffee the waitress had hurried to bring over. She took a swallow of the hot, black liquid and tried not to make a face. She really did hate coffee. Her usual breakfast consisted of fresh-squeezed orange juice; natural bran cereal, a supply of which she always carried with her when she was out on location; and goat's milk, picked up in a health-food store. Hotels were usually very accommodating in storing the milk in their kitchens. Cat had run out of supplies yesterday and had too many other things on her mind to remember to pick up more at the health-food store a few blocks away.

Now the idea of going back to that store, the same one at which she had bought the ingredients to make that special brew for Luke, felt too depressing. Anyway, she told herself, she wasn't one of those *fanatic* health-food nuts. Unfortunately, that brought to mind the dogless hot dog and beer she had with Luke on that moonlit cruise.

Dodger doctored his coffee with three miniature plastic containers of cream and two hefty teaspoons of sugar. He knew something pretty serious was up with Cat when she didn't break into a lecture about cholesterol. He wondered how a daughter he had raised alone from the time she was a tot could be so different from him in so many ways. Except when it came to being stubborn. That was one quality they shared.

"I hear you went off somewhere with Joanie Weston yesterday. Did you have a good time?" She never could let something sit.

Now there was another difference. Dodger was a very private man. Except for anger, mostly expressed on the job, he kept his emotions to himself. He especially made it a habit not to discuss the details of his personal life with Cat.

He had been, he admitted to himself, quite a chauvinist. He used to divide women into two categories—friends and sex objects. Maybe that was one reason he kept his relationships to himself. Cat, ever on guard against "male chauvinist pigs," would have lectured Dodger's ear off on the subject.

But now he was beginning to discover that some of his ideas were slowly changing. Joanie Weston was not a mere sex object, yet she was not simply a friend, either. He had not figured out exactly what she was. But he had no intention of sorting the matter out with his daughter.

"Well?" Cat insisted when Dodger remained silent.

"Well, what? Sure, I had a good time. No big

136

deal," he muttered. "And don't you go changing the subject."

"What subject?" she asked.

"The subject of why you didn't sleep last night. I hope Ben Seaton wasn't the cause," he said with a low growl.

"I thought you liked Ben." Good, she said to herself, he's off the track. Now to keep him there.

"Sure I like him. He drives me occasionally crazy with his derring-do, but he's a good kid and a top-notch stunter."

"So?"

"So—as a stunter, he's just fine. As a beau for my daughter, that's altogether different."

Cat laughed. "Beau? Oh, Dodger, you're too much. You go around looking like a thirty-year-old at the ripe old age of fifty-three and some of your ideas are as old as Grampa Roy rocking away on his porch down in Biloxi."

"Fifty-two. Don't you go rushing the years on me. They move along fast enough on their own."

A note of sadness underlying his typical gruff tone made Cat look up sharply. The idea of aging, another topic never discussed, was obviously bothering Dodger enough right now to let his feelings sneak to the surface. Cat wondered how much his interest in the young, attractive Joanie Weston had to do with this sudden concern. She reached out for his hand.

There were a lot of things she and her father didn't talk about, but there was a fierce bond of love and affection between them. They had weathered some tough storms together and Cat had, over the years, cast herself not only in the role of daughter, but as friend and helper as well. No matter what happened, they both knew they could always rely on each other.

Cat was sorely tempted to tell Dodger about Luke. Right now she needed somebody who could understand the whole thing—more than she could. But then Dodger returned to the subject of Ben Seaton and Cat lost her nerve.

"All your life you've been around stunters. Raised by one, too. Well, I never could talk you out of following in my footsteps, even though I still think it's a crazy enough life for a man, never mind a girl . . ."

Cat groaned.

"I know. I know. You think it's chauvinistic for me to want to see my daughter sitting in a little cottage surrounded by a white picket fence playing with her kids, bringing over her husband's pipe and slippers when he gets back from some nine-to-five job. Well, maybe it is. But maybe that little fantasy of mine for you is there 'cause I never had that kind of life, never gave you the chance to see if you might like it yourself."

Cat squeezed Dodger's hand. "Come on, Dad," she said softly, "you gave me the best upbringing a kid could have. Why, you gave me everything I ever wanted. Most important of all, you gave me your love."

Dodger cast his eyes down at his coffee. It would never do to start bawling.

Cat understood Dodger's silence and didn't push. When the waitress showed up with the food, he had pulled himself together. He even managed another wink at the waitress, who had brought him what appeared to be an extra large order of bacon and sausage.

Cat wasn't very hungry, but Dodger's hawklike vision seemed to be calculating every bite she took. If he thought her appetite was poor on top of her exhaustion, he would definitely get somebody else to do today's stunt work. Cat had not gotten where she was in the profession by copping out, for any reason, on her assignments. She was not about to let a couple of sleepless nights, both caused by Luke Eliot—his presence and then his absence—affect her work.

While they ate breakfast Dodger drew several diagrams on a small pad of paper to show Cat the changes he wanted to make in the chase sequence.

"I had the boys completely reinforce the carriage on the Corvette. Put in two steel templates on the driver's side, so only the passenger side would cave in on collision. I also had the front springs replaced with a stiffer set and switched to Koni shocks."

"You left the Mag wheels alone?"

Dodger nodded. "But the new shocks are going to alter the handling. We don't want the car leaping too high in the air when you take that dive off the ramp."

Cat agreed, studying the diagram of the chase as Dodger turned it to her.

"Now," he explained, "this is the only change. Instead of throwing clear of the car as it hits the bend in the road, I want you to break it into a right spin a hundred yards after that bend. That's the widest stretch of the road, and as you pull out of the spin, Ben will come up at your side. The camera will slide to him, and there's a nice soft shoulder with lots of extra dirt piled up to cushion you when you hit. It should go nice and easy, so you won't get any black and blues. At that spot we'll pick up shooting the dummy car. Ben will link his car to it and get it going for the grand finale."

"One of these days you're going to let me get in on that finale," Cat grumbled. Up to now that was one stunt Dodger had vetoed. It was just too risky, requiring someone with strength as well as ability. If the hydraulic pin that locked the dummy car's frame to the driver's car ever jammed, which had happened on a few occasions, the driver had to shove it manually. If he couldn't unlock his car from the other one, they would both be heading for that crash. Not only was the impact itself dangerous, but the dummy car was always fitted with explosives to make the crash that much more effective and spectacular.

"Let's not get into that again. You concentrate on your stunt and leave the rest up to the others."

Cat gave him a soldier's salute. At least he wasn't wavering about her performing today. She was glad she'd eaten her whole breakfast. Actually, she felt a little better.

140

Her improved mood lasted until Dodger cleared out to supervise one of Ben's stunts that morning. The movie they were shooting, a wild suspense yarn, had more than its share of work for stunters. Today Ben was going to be chased across rooftops and then beaten up by the bad guys. Cat had considered going along to watch, but she knew Dodger expected her to at least rest this morning, if not manage a real nap.

Sitting alone in the coffee shop, she stared at the torn-off sheet of paper Dodger had left for her to go over. As she tried to concentrate, she told herself that work was the only surefire way to get her mind off Luke. Ever since those two leaps out the window with Luke watching, she'd been having this fantasy that he'd continue to be around when she did the rest of her stunts. The idea was so comforting that it disturbed her.

Unlike a lot of stunters, Cat wasn't superstitious. Many of them carried special good-luck talismans with them when they performed—rabbit's feet, coins, religious medals—and Cat had seen them all. She had never needed a lucky charm before. Yet, in some ways, she had gotten it into her head that Luke's presence provided an almost magical effect. It was crazy. There was that word again. She scooped the paper into her pocket and walked out of the coffee shop.

An hour later, Cat was dutifully resting up in her hotel room when the phone rang.

"Cat, it's Joanie. Something's happened."

Cat immediately thought of Dodger. "What?"

141

she asked breathlessly, having leapt out of her bed, hand clutched to her stomach.

"It's Ben. He slipped on a patch of wet roof ledge and fell."

Cat's relief that Dodger was all right swiftly moved to a sick fear about Ben. "Is he— Is he . . ."

"He's unconscious. They've got him over at Mount Zion. Dodger's at the hospital along with most of the crew. He asked me to call and have you meet us over there."

"I'm on my way."

Fifteen minutes later, Cat was racing down the corridor of Mt. Zion toward her father and the others gathered in the small alcove. Dodger left the group and strode over to her, taking her by the shoulders so that she came to a sudden halt.

"Take it easy. He's going to be okay. This is one time that boy's hard head came in handy. He's got a slight concussion and a mighty healthy-size bump on the noggin, but otherwise he's still in one piece."

"Is he conscious?"

"And complaining to beat a band. Wants to leave his nice comfy bed and stalk some more rooftops. The doctor's keeping him flat on his back in the hospital for forty-eight hours. And then he doesn't recommend any heavy-duty gags for at least a week or two."

"But that's when the film wraps."

"Don't I know it. Bud and Leroy can pick up some of the slack. So can you."

Cat nodded enthusiastically.

"But I'd better try to get Drury or Spider down

for the tougher stunts and talk with Carl about rescheduling some of them. I just hope one of those guys is free."

Cat grabbed hold of his elbow as he started toward a phone a few yards down the hall. "Hold it a minute, Dodger. You're mostly worried about the crash today, right?"

"Not today, little girl. That's one rescheduling I've already taken care of. Turns out I don't have to worry about you being wide-awake enough to handle your gag today after all."

"When is it rescheduled for?"

"Tentatively, Wednesday. If I get one of my boys."

"How about your girl?" She tugged on his sleeve as he shook his head. "Come on, Dodger. I can do it. You know I can. I'm going to try that stunt one of these days, anyway—with or without your consent."

"Not while you're on my crew, you're not."

"I don't always work for you, Dodger."

"Well, then do it somewhere else. I'm not having it on my conscience if anything happens to you 'cause I let you do something I didn't think you could handle. And since I'm pretty tight with most other head stunt men, I don't think you'll be testing your wings in that direction for quite a while."

Cat glared angrily, her eyes almost black. "You are impossible. I know the risks. I also know I'm damn strong and levelheaded enough to handle things if an emergency . . . You aren't even listening," she snapped as Dodger turned to go.

143

"This here's a hospital, little girl. They've got sick people."

In a low, tight voice Cat said, "Don't call me little girl."

Dodger chuckled, completely deflating Cat's fury, and walked over to the phone. Cat joined the others, noticing as she drew near that Joanie's eyes kept shifting to the phone where Dodger was making his calls.

A couple of minutes later, Dodger, looking none too happy, sauntered over.

"No luck?" Joanie was the first to speak.

Dodger looked over at her and then shot a quick glance at Cat. He shook his head.

"How about Royce?" someone else suggested.

"Busted arm. Drury told me."

The doctor who was treating Ben came over to give them an update.

"Can my daughter go in and see him?" Dodger asked.

"Sure. It will probably do Mr. Seaton some good." The doctor eyed Cat appreciatively, his point clearly made.

Cat wasn't sure whether Dodger was still under the misconception that she and Ben had something going or whether he just wanted to keep her from pursuing her argument about doing the crash. Now that he couldn't get someone else, he was going to have to choose from those on hand. He may have put an end to her arguing for now, but it was only temporary. She smiled sweetly at Dodger and walked down to Ben's room.

144

"I don't know why, Doctor, but I just never seem to pick them right." Adrienne Vaughn sighed, staring from Luke to the colorful glass paperweight on his desk. She'd been seeing Dr. Eliot for three months now about the problem of her disastrous relationships with men. "Do you think I'm scared of intimacy or something? I read an article in *Cosmo* the other day that said that's the underlying reason behind most failed marriages."

"What do you think about the article?" Luke was always the psychiatrist—question for question.

Adrienne grinned. She was a bright, reasonably attractive thirty-two-year-old woman who understood that the therapy process was always directed toward encouraging the patient to come up with the answers. "I think *Cosmo* has a point. I get this funny feeling in my gut sometimes when I'm with a guy I've seen for more than a few times, and—and these sort of nutty questions start running through my mind."

"What questions?"

"Silly things like, does he remember to cap the toothpaste after he's used it? Does he leave his clothes lying around the floor when he gets undressed? More general issues, too, like, will he love me with curlers in my hair or when I'm sick? Will he still bring me flowers in ten years? Will we have anything to talk about a year from now?" her voice dropped. "Will he be faithful? That's always a big one."

"None of those questions sound silly to me.

145

They seem quite important. Maybe being able to answer them is the secret of working out the problems you have with men."

"I'm trying to do that now with Michael. We've had only a few dates, so I can't even begin to answer most of those questions. Really, all I know right now is that I'm wildly attracted to him. But he's so different from me in so many ways— politically, socially . . . He's even in a bowling league!" She smiled, her eyes flashing down to her watch to see that her time was just about up. "On the other hand, most of the men I have more in common with bore me silly. Tell me, Doctor, do you believe the saying, 'Opposites attract'?"

"It's certainly one that has been around for a long time." He smiled back as he stood up, signaling the end of their session.

Adrienne Vaughn rose. "Yeah, but how long does that attraction last?" She didn't expect an answer to the question, any more than she ever did, but it was one she sure would have liked someone to be able to tell her.

When his patient left, Luke's smile vanished. These past few days it seemed like every patient had brought up issues he could connect to his relationship with Cat. He had put all of his energy into his work as a way to stop thinking about her, and the plan had completely backfired.

Luke was tired, on edge; he hadn't taken a single note for his book in days; he'd burned the toast every morning so far this week, and it was only Wednesday. It was also only three days since he'd kissed Cat good-bye. It felt like a lifetime—a lifetime of missing her.

Two o'clock. His last patient had cancelled and he was through for the day. He called in to his answering service for messages. Nothing pressing from patients, but there were two calls from Teri. He hesitated, then dialed her office number. Teri must have told her secretary to put through his call immediately.

"Hi, stranger. You didn't return my call yesterday," Teri quipped.

Luke had pushed that message aside. "Tuesday's my tightest day, Teri. I'm lucky if I get time to grab a bite to eat or run to the bathroom."

"I wanted to see how you were feeling and find out whether we're still on for Friday."

"Friday? Oh, right. The Alcoholism Seminar at General. Yes, I'm still planning on it." He idly browsed through the newspaper on his desk as he spoke. Usually he read it first thing, but he had scheduled an appointment for seven this morning and hadn't had time to do more than scan the front page.

"Great. Why don't you come over for dinner first and then we'll go to the meeting together?" Her tone was casual, but Luke knew she would be hurt if he turned down her offer again. On the other hand, he did not want to give off misleading messages.

"I tell you what. Fridays I work till six. How about meeting me across the street for dinner at the Magic Pan and I'll take you up on your offer of homecooking another time?"

He heard an almost inaudible sigh and then her acquiescence. As he was about to hang up, Teri broke in. "By the way, guess who I ran into on my rounds yesterday at Mount Zion?"

"Who?"

"Your stunt friend."

"Cat?" The note of concern rang through sharply.

"Don't worry. She wasn't in a hospital bed. One of her pals fell off a roof and she was visiting him."

"Fell off a roof?"

"I told you that was a dangerous profession. The man was lucky. It was just a minor concussion, although how he didn't kill himself is beyond me."

"Is he a powerful-looking guy in his forties with dark—"

"He's thirty at the most. My guess is more like twenty-six, twenty-seven. Blond and extremely handsome. Your friend obviously thinks so, too. They were in a rather passionate embrace when I walked in with my group for rounds."

"Really," was all Luke could manage to eke out. One of her "kissing cousins" no doubt. "That was my buzzer for my next appointment," he lied. "I'll speak to you later."

The newspaper was turned to the entertainment pages. As Luke started to close the paper and get ready to go home, he noticed a caption about a new film being shot in the city. He knew, without reading the article, that it had to be Cat's picture. San Francisco had grown popular for location shooting, but the likelihood of more than one film being shot at a time here was improbable.

There was a list by day of where *Dangerous Assignment* was being filmed. On Wednesday there was going to be a chase sequence in and around the Embarcadero area.

Luke told himself there was less point than ever in seeing Cat again. What if Teri had been right? What if she had something going with this man in the hospital? As well as with the tall, handsome, gray-haired guy. Maybe she had just sandwiched him in for the night between the two of them.

His office on Geary Street was nowhere near the Embarcadero. He had no excuse for "being in the neighborhood." He couldn't even use the excuse that he wanted to tell Cat Roy off. Their one madly beautiful night together gave him no claims on her.

The hell with excuses. The truth was, he had to see her again and he could not think beyond that need.

Luke had no trouble finding the set. Quite a few people had already gathered to watch. The action was taking place on a street corner where Liz Fuller and an actor Luke did not recognize were busy arguing for the cameras. As Luke wandered down the street to where two cars for the film were being given the once-over, he spied another argument going on, this one not part of the film.

It was Cat and the tall, dark-haired guy going at it tooth and nail. They didn't spot him, and he couldn't make out what they were saying, but he

149

could see the glint of determination in Cat's eyes and the sharply etched frown of frustration on the man's brow. Finally, the man threw up his hands and walked over to a mechanic rolling out from under the car. That was when Cat saw Luke.

She started toward him. Her face was flushed with excitement, but Luke wasn't sure whether or not he was the cause. He didn't get an opportunity to find out. She was called back to get ready to shoot. Cat threw him a kiss and shouted for him to wait for her as she hurried over to the car.

What a day, she thought exuberantly. Not only had Dodger finally consented, albeit reluctantly, to letting her do the crash, after making her manually remove that damn hydraulic pin a dozen times, but her very special lucky charm had reappeared.

Cat slipped her visor over her face and zipped herself into her special asbestos suit. This was an extra precaution. The point was for her to do this part of the stunt without getting anywhere near the exploding car.

Yesterday she had shot the original part of her sequence—the one Dodger had gone over with her on Monday morning. This afternoon she was taking Ben's place at the wheel for the big finale. Her anticipation and excitement were really flying now that Luke was watching. He'd shown up just when she had finally decided she couldn't stand not seeing him again and was getting up her nerve to call him that night. Now she wouldn't have to make that call.

Luke stood on the sidelines, close to a couple of the mechanics. One of them had noticed Cat's gesture toward Luke and came over to him.

"Is Cat a friend of yours?"

"We met a few days ago."

"Ever see someone do a crash gag before?"

"Gag?"

"Stunt. In the business we call it a gag."

"Oh," Luke said, feeling all the more a complete outsider.

"I sure hope she can handle this one. Our guy got himself a concussion the other day, and Cat finally talked the boss into letting her handle it."

"How dangerous is it?" Luke felt a large lump in his throat.

"Well, let's just say that if everything goes according to plan it will be a breeze."

"If it doesn't . . . ?" He didn't really want to hear the answer.

"She could either get herself burned up bad or smashed to smithereens. Don't worry, though," he said to Luke, who was rapidly turning a strong shade of green beside him. "Cat Roy is a pro. And really, all she has to do to stay perfectly safe is to pull that release. Handling the car for the slow-down is a cinch. You watch her handle this baby."

It was the last thing in the world Luke wanted to do, but he felt riveted to the spot. He stood there watching her car and the empty duplicate Corvette, attached in some way he couldn't exactly figure out, speeding up as they headed straight toward a large brick wall. A sharp wave of nausea

151

attacked his stomach. Seconds before the cars were going to hit the wall, the empty car shot forward on its own, slammed onto the wall, and exploded in a burst of flames. The other car had come to a stop a few yards away. Cat had been so quick to escape before the explosion sent debris flying that Luke never saw her until the flames subsided.

Cat yanked the helmet off as several crew members ran up to congratulate her on a perfectly executed stunt. When she finally broke free of the group and turned in Luke's direction, he was nowhere in sight.

"Hey, Bob, where did that guy go that you were talking to?"

"He left in a hurry. I think that gag did it for his stomach."

CHAPTER NINE

Dodger stood off to the sidelines while the others gathered around Cat. When they went off, he walked over to her, wanting to offer his congratulations alone.

"You did a good job there, little girl."

"Good? I did a great job and you know it, you old codger." Cat was still distracted by Luke's disappearance, but she gave her father a wide grin. Dodger didn't throw compliments around, and she was particularly happy with this one. She gave her father a big bear hug.

"Well, wasn't I great?" she asked, giving him a nudge in the stomach with her helmet.

Dodger grabbed it and plunked it back on her head. "Just be sure your head doesn't get so big that this won't fit on the next time around."

"Gotcha, boss." She grinned.

"And, Cat, don't start believing it's all easy sailing from here on out. Ben is still my number-one pick for this gag."

"Ben might fall off another roof," she teased. "Don't worry, Dodger, I'll wait my turn in line. I don't mind as long as I know I'm not waiting in vain."

"I see a lot of people in this business getting so high on their abilities that they begin to think they're indestructible. I don't want to see that happen to you. The cemeteries are packed with those people." Dodger's gaze reflected pain and anger.

Cat put her arms around Dodger's neck. "I'm going to be okay, Dodger. This head of mine doesn't swell easily."

He ruffled her hair, wanting to ease the intensity of the moment. "See that you keep it that way. I plan to dance at your wedding—and at my grandchildren's as well."

Another topic rarely discussed. Not that Cat wasn't absolutely clear on the issues. Dodger wanted Cat married, out of the business, and settled down with a houseful of kids. What Cat didn't know was that lately Dodger was acutely aware of how much he regretted not having that kind of life himself. At some point he was going to have to talk with Cat about Joanie. First, he needed to be sure there really was something to talk about.

"Oh, Dodger, about dinner tonight . . ." Cat scanned the area again for Luke. She was sure he'd be back. Bob might not have been joking when he'd said Luke had run off looking green. He could have gotten a little overwhelmed watching the gag. Even knowing she was only doing a stunt was likely to be a little unsettling to someone who wasn't in the business. It was something she was sure he'd get used to in time.

For the past couple of nights, after visiting Ben at the hospital, Cat and Dodger had stopped off at a restaurant for dinner. Today Ben was back at the hotel convalescing.

"Listen, Cat, do you mind if I beg off tonight? I've got a lot of work to do," Dodger said.

"Planning to go over some special effects?" she teased. The idea of Dodger and Joanie was beginning to feel less uncomfortable to Cat. Anyway, she thought, it's most likely another of Dodger's brief involvements. She only hoped Joanie was looking at it the same way. Cat was very fond of Joanie and didn't want to see her get hurt.

Dodger flushed, his gaze directed somewhere between his shoes, hers, and the pavement. Cat began to wonder if she was assessing the situation correctly.

She put Dodger's love life out of her mind. Hoping to spend the evening with Luke, she told her father she didn't mind dining without him tonight.

She hung around the area after the crew had cleared up the debris and gone off. Her initial optimism that Luke would show up again took a complete nosedive when nearly twenty minutes went by and there was no sign of him. Why had he shown up in the first place? Curiosity? One last look? She was leaving on Monday. Maybe he'd come over to say good-bye again and then decided against it.

Cat never did like other people making decisions that affected her without some of her own input. As she stalked back to her dressing area, she decided that she had some very definite points of her own to make, and she had no intention of letting Luke wander off into the blue without his knowing what they were.

She had just pulled off one of the toughest daredevil stunts in the business. So why not another, she mused with a smile.

Liz Fuller was removing her makeup in her dressing room.

"Well, if it isn't Wonder Woman herself." Liz grinned. "You know, I tried to talk Dodger out of letting you do that crazy gag. What would I do if I lost the best double I ever had?"

Cat came over to the dressing table. "Thanks a lot. And I thought you loved me for me alone."

Liz squeezed her knee. "We'll be pals all the way to the Hollywood Haven Rest Home for ancient actors and busted-up old stunters."

"I thought we could be pals all the way to Rome," Cat said, dabbing her finger into some cold cream and rubbing it across her dried lips. She may have appeared cool as a cucumber before that stunt today, but contrary to Liz's comment, she wasn't Wonder Woman. She had stepped into that Corvette fully cognizant of the risks. Now she was stepping into another risky situation, and this time she was far less certain of the actual dangers involved.

Her feelings baffled her. In the past she was always the one angling to keep relationships casual, making sure she didn't get herself tangled up so tightly that she wouldn't be able to undo the knots. Now she was throwing the lasso over herself with her own two hands. Rome meant Greece. And Greece meant Luke. This was some crazy stunt she was embarking on. She could be heading for the biggest crash of her life. Then again, Cat was very accomplished at pulling up the brakes when danger came close to disaster.

"Well, pack your bags, sweetie. We head out one week from today. Dodger's got the whole schedule. You'll be happy to hear you are going to get that opportunity to loll around the Greek islands for a while. Peter ordered some last-minute rewrites, and there's going to be an extra week location shooting on Skiathos and some of the other little islands in that area. I hope I can handle it." Liz stared at her image in the mirror.

"The ghost of Tony Vargos?" Cat asked gently.

Liz turned to Cat. "I did what may turn out to be a very dumb thing. I asked Peter to audition Tony for a small part in *Victims*."

"And he got it."

Liz nodded, a sly grin forming. "I started remembering those romantic nights with Tony on that yacht and how good we were together. . . .

Now that I've gone and set myself up, I'm beginning to remember all the problems."

Cat sighed. "Look, all you're doing is giving yourself a second chance. What if you and Tony could make a go of it again?" What if Luke and I could? She had to talk to somebody. She and Liz were now in the same boat. They were both about to do something that could be very dumb.

"Liz, if I talk to you about something—something personal, do you promise you won't laugh or—or . . ."

"Of course not, Cat. We joked around before about being pals, but I could use a friend to confide in, and if you could, too, I'd love it."

Cat moved away from the table and began to pace the small trailer dressing room.

"Remember the doctor that tried to stop me from jumping out of that window?" She saw Liz nod and went on. "Well, I've seen him again. That afternoon I went over to his apartment. I was just going to apologize." She paused. "No, I wasn't. I wanted to see him again.

"Something crazy happened to me up on that ledge." She gave Liz a sly smile. "It felt almost like a bolt of electricity went through me. He looked at me with those sexy eyes of his, and I felt like I was melting inside. It wasn't only a physical attraction. There was something about him—a gentleness, a sincerity, a feeling that people really mattered to him, that I mattered. It really shook me, Liz. Maybe I went back to see him to prove to myself I'd let my imagination get carried away. Only it didn't work out that way."

Liz smiled. "How did it work out?"

"We spent the next evening and night together." Cat stopped pacing. "We told ourselves and each other that it was fantasy—one special night of love and then back to our real lives."

"You don't want the fantasy to end?"

"That's the problem." Cat perched herself on the dressing table's edge. "Does it have to be a fantasy? Is it so impossible for the two of us to have something real?" She cast Liz a wan smile. "It probably is impossible." She remembered Luke's little speech in her hotel room after she'd pulled that stunt with the bellhop. If he ever did settle down it was going to be with a woman like Teri Caulfield, someone who matched his life-style.

"Where does Greece fit into all of this?" Liz asked.

"Luke is going to be there this summer. Maybe my taking on this film is a dumb idea."

"Oh, no. You aren't backing out now. If you can tell me to take the risk of a second go-around with Tony, then the same is true for you, sweetie. Besides, we'll each have a friendly shoulder to cry on if things don't work out."

Cat dipped her pinky finger in Liz's pot of rouge, smeared one spot on her own forehead, one smudge on Liz's. "There, now we're blood sisters."

When Luke reached his apartment, he walked into the living room and sank into the couch. That stunt of Cat's really had done a number on his stomach, but his head felt even worse. What had ever possessed him to think there was any way he could contend with someone like Cat Roy, a woman who came within a hair's breadth of killing herself every time she went off to work? When she wasn't leaping out of windows, she was steering into brick walls. And this was only one film. He realized he'd seen the barest fraction of what her life was all about. But he'd seen enough to know it wasn't for him.

One issue resolved. That left the burning passion still ripping a hole through his heart. Seeing her again had not helped that issue. Instead it had made the flames shoot out more fiercely.

He walked into the kitchen and made himself a cup of tea. His eyes drifted to the window. He went back into the living room, determined to forget phantom images. Sitting at his desk, he made an effort to organize some of his notes. The pamphlets on Greece were cast off to one side.

He picked up a letter confirming his cottage for the month of July on the isle of Skiathos off the coast of Athens. He had picked this little island as his headquarters after weeks of research and talks with travel agents. Not only was it supposed to be very beautiful with its wild strawberry bushes, forests of olive trees, and silver-pebbled beaches, but it had easy access to Athens and ferry service to the other outlying islands in the chain.

Why couldn't he focus on his trip instead of on Cat? Before she appeared on that ledge, his fantasies had easily slipped into ones of Greece, even to meeting some exotic Mediterranean beauty there for a brief but satisfying interlude. Now those fantasies eluded him.

His doorbell rang. As he walked across the living room he saw a note being slipped under the door. He bent to pick it up. As he unfolded the paper he opened the door. There was no one there. Standing in the hallway, he glanced down at the neat, angular script and the big, bold signature.

The note was brief: "Sorry you couldn't wait for me this afternoon. I wanted you to meet Dodger, the guy I told you was like family to me. Actually, he is family. He's been bossing me around since I was a baby."

Cat popped out of her hiding place around the corner. She held out a familiar-looking Thermos. "Dumb excuse, huh?" She grinned.

"I'm glad you came up with some reason to reappear." He walked slowly over to her.

"This time I filled it with my secret stomach-settler recipe. Bob said you looked kind of green when you left the shoot."

"I don't need it now."

"What do you need?" she whispered against his ear as he moved closer.

He smiled. "I may need to be committed in the morning, but at this moment all I need—all I want—is you."

"Don't worry, Doc," she said in that hot, sultry voice that moved right through him, "I only want to drive you a little crazy." She slid her arms around his neck as he lifted her in his arms, carrying her back to the apartment.

Luke slammed his door shut with his foot and walked into the living room. He didn't put Cat down, not wanting to let go of her now that he had her in his arms again. She felt so vital, so good, so full of life and energy. It was hard to even remember his fears as he pressed her against him. The pain seemed so removed from the ecstasy of the moment.

Cat loved the way he held her—like she was the most precious thing that he'd ever carried. She circled his neck in a tighter clasp, content to stay where she was.

Luke moved to the couch, sat down with Cat on his lap. Her eyes were a bright sea-blue as she gazed at him.

She leaned forward to kiss him, but he held her at arm's length, his eyes narrowing. "Family—huh?"

"Dear old dad," she acknowledged, her eyes glimmering.

"I wouldn't call him old. I hope I look that good when I have a daughter your age. How old are you, anyway? Do you realize how little I actually know about you?"

"I'm old enough to know what I'm doing," she murmured seductively, kissing him lightly.

Luke cupped her chin. "Any other family I ought to know about? Like that guy in the hospital who fell off a roof?"

"Teri talked with you about him, huh?"

"Not only about him. She said the two of you were quite chummy when she came into his room. Is he a brother?" he asked skeptically.

"No. And he's not a kissing cousin, either. Just a friend. And speaking of friends—how about Teri?"

"Just a friend." He grinned.

"Then I guess we're both presently unattached," she said in that low, husky voice that drove him to distraction.

He kissed her with deliberate slowness, savoring the sweet taste of her lips, the faint scent of wild-flower shampoo as her hair fell against her face. She returned the kiss, teasing his tongue with hers, so that he pulled her harder against him.

Cat slid her hand inside his shirt, pressing her palm against his heart. He kissed her again, his hands sliding down her back, tugging her shirt out of the waistband of her jeans, so that he could feel the silky, smooth texture of her skin.

Luke intentionally kept a languid pace, despite the torture to his senses and to his body. He had to make this moment last. Cat's appearance was only a brief reprieve, and he meant to savor these few extra, precious moments to the fullest. The pain of tomorrow seemed a small price to pay for the experience of being with her today. Even if he thought differently when he watched her walk out the door the next morning, he knew he would never regret what was happening.

Cat was in no hurry, either. But her reasons were different. To her this was the beginning, not the end, of their relationship, and there was no need to frantically capture one last moment. She intended to capture many more in Greece.

As Luke slowly, methodically began unbuttoning her shirt, she let herself fall back onto the couch, making it easier for him. Her pose so reminded him of that first afternoon when she'd stretched out in the same provocative way that he had to laugh.

"What's the joke?"

"No joke," he said, bending over to kiss the tip of her nose. "Did you know that I wanted to ravage you that first afternoon in my apartment? I kept checking my robe to make sure I wasn't giving myself away."

Cat laughed. "I wish I'd been more attentive. I was too busy trying to contend with my own wild passion. Especially after you kissed me. You are a terrific kisser."

"Only that?" He nibbled her neck so that she giggled.

"Stop. I'm very ticklish."

"Never," he mumbled into her ear, continuing his foray.

"Never?" She edged away.

Luke stopped then. He looked down at her. He never did want to stop, but he knew that was part of the fantasy. Another part of that fantasy was not letting reality intrude. Yet Cat's question was too real to ignore.

Luke moved his hand away from the small of her back and sat up. Cat didn't move.

164

For a few minutes neither of them spoke. Then Luke reached out for her hand, lacing her fingers with his.

"Cat, I wish things were simple. Those are foolish words from a psychiatrist who knows life is anything but."

"Maybe we'd better talk about the complications," Cat said, sitting up beside Luke.

"I don't want to talk about complications or even think about them," he said, giving her a sheepish grin. "I want to pretend there aren't any, so that I can make love to you without admitting it's going to end. I want to forget for the moment that in a little while you are going to walk out of my life and it will be over."

"Does it have to be over?" She felt an icy shiver go through her as she waited for his answer. She wasn't even certain what answer she wanted. All she knew was that she was not ready to say goodbye to Luke and walk out of his life forever.

He stared down at their hands, still intertwined. "Don't think I haven't had fantasies about that. The problem is, I can never get very far with them. First, there's the logistics of the whole thing. You aren't about to hang around San Francisco, and I'm not going to traipse around the globe waiting while you finish crashing up some car or other. You would feel totally foreign in my world, Cat. You would think it positively dull. And I feel like an alien in yours. More than that. It terrifies me. I couldn't cope with it."

"I could never give it up, Luke. Any more than I'd ever ask you to give up your life."

"There it is—the same stalemate I come up with in my fantasies. Don't you see, Cat, neither of us wants to give up what we have, and that's only right." He pulled her to him. "I also don't want to give you up, but I don't honestly see any way around it."

Cat decided this was definitely not the time to tell Luke she was going to be in Greece. He was ambivalent enough, determined to keep the relationship under tight control. It wasn't that what Luke said didn't make sense. She'd said the same things to herself right up to the moment she rang his bell. But when they were together like this, she felt capable of surmounting any obstacles.

"You don't have to give me up this moment." She kissed him lightly. "I never did believe in worrying about tomorrow. Besides"—she bent low, her half-unbuttoned blouse revealing irresistible treasures—"if you send me away, I might do somthing rash, like jump out of a window."

"Please," he whispered, his hand slipping under her blouse, "don't do that."

"It's nice to know someone cares enough to want to save a total stranger." She grinned.

"You're not a stranger. I feel like I know you— very well." He stood up and stretched out his hand to her. "Here, give me your hand. I'll help you."

She placed her hand in his. "You really think I

have something to offer, Doc?" she teased, playing that first scene on the ledge all the way through.

Luke laughed. "Definitely. I can say that from experience."

"Well," she said, and sighed, "they're forecasting a damp, cold night. As you once said, it's a lousy time for jumping. Anyway, I think your idea makes a lot more sense."

The fantasy was again intact as Luke took Cat in his arms. He kissed her deeply, then held her away from him for a moment to feast his eyes on her. An electric current coursed through him as he slipped her shirt off. She wasn't wearing anything underneath it. She gave him a wicked little smile. He reached for the waistband of her jeans, unzipping them to see that she had not bothered with any underthings.

"You told me I was wanton," she murmured in a breathy voice.

He kissed her breasts, his hands cupping them tenderly. "My beautiful wanton tiger." A rush of excitement sped through his veins as she undid the catch on his trousers, slipping her hand inside.

Her eyes were dark, the look she gave him part mischief, part passion. She was intoxicating, her touch driving him wild. Without releasing him, her other hand deftly unbuttoned his shirt, her lips and tongue branding him with her special heat.

"If you keep this up, we're never going to make it to the bedroom," he whispered, and then moaned as she slid to her knees, her tongue trailing a burning path downward. She tugged off the rest of his clothes, then gripped his knees, causing him to tumble down on top of her.

"We can move to the bedroom later," she said, stretching out on the soft shag carpet.

Luke took her jeans off as Cat arched her back to help him. It was a deliciously seductive pose, and Luke took full advantage of it. Again he was struck by her utter sensuousness, her natural abandon. He loved the way she gasped with pleasure, openly expressing her joy at his caresses, giving herself so freely to his explorations, creating some of her own.

He had known other women, experienced other pleasures, but there was no one in the world like Cat. He felt consumed with the fire she sparked in him, loving the way she fueled the flames with her touches, her whispered words of longing, her moans of excitement as they caressed each other.

She sat up, folding her legs beneath her, perching back on her heels. Her eyes closed, the dark lashes fluttering against her cheeks as Luke reached out, tracing a line from the valley between her breasts to the heart of her passion. She arched her back as his tongue followed the same path, searching out the source of her fire. She parted her lips, her whole body trembling, submitting to his quest. Her hand moved over his firm back. Cat could feel the ripple of his muscles as she stroked him.

He pressed his lips along her inner thighs, then eased her back down on the carpet. Her legs entwined around him as he moved on top of her. She clung to him as the power of her need escalated, the rhythmic undulation of their bodies exquisitely in tune. She cried out his name as she reached the peak of pleasure, a single teardrop rolling down her cheek. He captured it with his lips, tasting the salty tang, then shared it with her as he kissed her lips.

She loved the feeling of intimacy as he cradled her to him after they made love, his lips pressed to her hair, his hands idly stroking her back and breasts.

"This is the best feeling in the world," she said, then laughed. "No, the second best."

Luke kissed her brow. He started to say, the best is yet to come. Funny how he kept thinking into the future, when he'd already made it clear there wasn't any real future to be had.

CHAPTER TEN

From the time the cast and crew had arrive in Rome to their touchdown at the Ellinikon Airport in Greece, tensions had run high. Stepping out of the air-conditioned terminal, the heat of the mid-morning sun engulfed the small group. Cat hoisted her backpack over her shoulders, wiping the perspiration from her forehead. She could hear disgruntled comments from the others as they gathered up their luggage and paraphernalia. The weather was not going to help cool people's tempers.

To begin with, everyone was annoyed at Peter Whitney. The thirty-two-year-old director might be a film genius, but he was erratic, demanding, and frequently infuriating. He had also gone through four scriptwriters and two assistant directors in less than a month. Cat was definitely not going to give him her vote for Mr. Congeniality, and she doubted anyone else would, either. Especially Dodger.

Peter and her father had not agreed on one single execution of a stunt, and considering this was a film containing a large number of gags, the war was just starting. Cat had a feeling, however, that Dodger's tense mood was not only due to his aggravating encounters with Peter Whitney, who so far had backed down on his demands, letting Dodger ultimately have his way. There was a more subtle strain between Dodger and Joanie Weston, who had signed up at the last minute to work on the film. Cat was pretty sure Dodger and Joanie had gone their separate ways personally, but she sensed that neither of them was too happy about the decision. A couple of times, when Cat had broached the subject with him, Dodger had nearly bitten off her head. Joanie had been equally testy whenever Cat mentioned Dodger.

And then there was Liz Fuller and Tony Vargos. The first week of shooting in Rome, the two of them had been inseparable. Then followed two weeks of Cat lending Liz her shoulder for frequent cries as her friend's fantasy started to come undone.

Tony resented what he saw as his second-class status on the film. He found it equally hard to accept Liz's star billing. From that conflict flowed many others. Tony still had a wandering eye for a pretty girl in a bikini; Liz seemed too chummy with Ned Weeks, her co-star. Both Liz and Tony fought with Whitney, but even there they couldn't get together, each feeling the other's arguments were not the important issues.

What it boiled down to was that they had reached a point where the only thing they shared was the mutual need to keep the fight going. It was beginning to wear on everybody. And Cat's shoulder was getting waterlogged.

Liz caught up with Cat as they boarded the bus that would take them to the Hotel Hermes in the old section of Athens. They would be staying in the city for a couple of days to rest up before they ferried over to Alonnisos where they were setting up a home base.

Alonnisos was in the Sporades islands, as was Skiathos, the island, which by Cat's calculations, Luke should be on. The only problem was, having witnessed the brief ups and the skyrocketing downs of two other romances these past few weeks, Cat was no longer sure she should even see him. Her initial confidence about working out some kind of a relationship with Luke was fast waning.

"Don't panic." Liz smiled as she fell in step with Cat. "I'm all cried out. Besides, I am so ecstatic about having two days off from battling dear, sweet Peter that nothing could upset my apple cart."

"Great," Cat said cheerfully. Her smile faded as they passed Tony Vargos, who was having an intimate little tête-à-tête with the airline stewardess from their Rome flight. She shot a quick glance at Liz to see her reaction.

Liz gave Tony a cool stare and walked faster. Cat hurried to catch up.

"Remember, nothing is going to upset your apple cart," Cat whispered.

"You're right," Liz said with a determined shake of her head. "While you're reminding me of things, would you also remind me never again to act out on a dumb fantasy? I wish I hadn't gotten him that audition."

Cat didn't respond. She was thinking about her own fantasy. It was beginning to seem far more implausible than Liz's. At least Tony and Liz had shared a profession. Then again, that seemed to be the main source of contention between them. Cat was thoroughly confused. Maybe a couple of days relaxing in Athens would help her decide what to do about Luke.

Liz picked up on Cat's mood. "Hey, just because my fantasy didn't work out doesn't mean yours is dumb."

"Dumber," Cat muttered. "Luke's probably forgotten all about me. Chalked me up as a nice little interlude—great research for his book."

Liz gave Cat's shoulder an affectionate squeeze. Cat had told her about Luke's treatise on sexual fulfillment. "If it was that good between the two of you that he wants to use it in his book, you'd better believe he has not forgotten—anything."

Cat grinned. "It was good. And I'm not just referring to physical gratification. I wish I knew what to do, Liz."

"I'm not a great one to be giving advice, but I'd say you were really hooked on the guy. The only way you're going to find out if there's anything real about your fantasy is to see him again."

Peter Whitney was waiting for Liz at the bus. Liz groaned. "If he has one more rewrite for me to memorize, I am going to take that man and drop him off Mount Olympus."

Liz greeted Peter with a forced smile. He laughed. "No rewrites, I promise."

Cat patted Peter on the back. "Good thing. Liz, here, was about to teach you a new stunt I was telling her about—it involves a long fall off a short cliff."

"Speaking of stunts"—Peter put his hands on Cat's shoulders—"would you please talk some sense into Dodger? That deep-sea dive is not going to be effective if you're wearing that tank suit."

"Dodger isn't out to protect his daughter's virtue," Cat said with a broad smile. Peter had wanted her to take that dive in the nude but had begrudgingly agreed to a skimpy bikini. Cat had been willing, but Dodger had been adamant about her using a full one-piece suit with some hidden padding. "The impact on the body from that height can be pretty rough. The suit will at least protect some vital parts," she said pointedly.

"You've done those dives in bikinis in other films," Peter argued, "and you still look pretty damned good to me."

"Dodger wasn't my boss on those films, Peter."

Peter shrugged, knowing he wasn't going to win on this one. They would have to do some fancy cutting so that the dreadful black tank suit did not stand out.

"Cheer up, Peter," Liz said as Tony nudged past them and boarded the bus. "How about letting me buy you some dinner tonight and we can drown our woes in a large bottle of ouzo?"

"My mouth is already watering," he said with a playful leer. Or was it playful? Neither Cat nor Liz was altogether sure. Peter's green eyes had a distinct glimmer as he helped Liz up the steps of the bus.

Cat smiled to herself as Liz and Peter slipped into a double seat in the back of the bus. Some folks healed rapidly when their fantasies fell through. She envied people like that.

Cat took a seat next to Joanie, who was still reading the same novel she had started weeks ago in Rome. Cat wondered if she was still on the same page.

"Good book?" Cat asked as she settled her backpack under the seat.

Joanie, not looking up, muttered, "Yes."

A few minutes later, after Cat noticed Joanie had not turned a page, she asked, "Do you have plans for dinner tonight? I thought maybe we could hit the town together. Unless you're hitting it with someone else?"

Joanie looked away from her book then and stared out the window as the bus bumped down the narrow street. She brushed a damp strand of brown hair from her face. The air conditioning on the bus barely made a dent in the intense morning heat.

"I don't have any plans for dinner tonight," Joanie said softly, a note of sadness in her tone. She turned to Cat. "Sure, let's paint the town red. I'm getting pretty tired of the color blue." She made an effort to smile, but Cat could tell it wasn't easy.

As they continued in silence for the rest of the ride, Joanie again buried her face in her book, hardly ever turning the pages. Cat spotted Dodger glancing over at them several times, then abruptly turning back around. She was pretty sure he wasn't checking on her.

Love, Cat thought derisively, who needs it? She dozed off until the bus pulled up to the hotel.

The Hermes was quite full, and although Cat would have preferred a single room, she readily agreed to double with Joanie.

"Sorry about that," Joanie said as they rode up together in the elevator.

"It will be more fun this way," Cat said lightly.

For an answer, she received a doubtful glance from Joanie.

The room was one of the more modern motel-type varieties. Had they not been in Greece, they could have been in any of those pull-off-the-road motels that dotted the major highways across the States. But it was clean and large enough for two people not to feel crowded in. And if it wasn't for the building across the street, they would have had a fabulous view of the Acropolis.

Cat decided to shower and then go to the roof garden of the hotel to see if there was a better view from there. She invited Joanie along but received a lethargic shake of the head.

"I know," Cat teased good-naturedly, "you just can't put that book of yours down. Well, I won't bug you, but you'd better not back down on our plans for tonight."

Joanie smiled. "I promise."

As Cat started for the bathroom, Joanie added, "I appreciate your tact."

"I only wish I understood why I needed it," Cat said with a shrug.

"Maybe we can talk about it tonight."

Cat nodded. She took her shower, and when she stepped back in the bedroom, Joanie was gone. She decided to skip the roof garden's possible view of the Acropolis for the real thing.

A few years ago, when she had been in Greece on another picture, she had loved going there early in the morning just as the gates were opening. It was empty and relatively cool at that time of day.

Dressed in a white handkerchief cotton sundress, comfortable low-heeled sandals, and a large, floppy white straw sun hat, Cat did not find the afternoon heat oppressive. The almost empty streets attested to the fact that most other people did.

She stopped at a small taverna along one of the narrow roads that ultimately led to the Acropolis and had a light lunch. A distinguished, middle-aged gentleman, sitting alone at another table, smiled as Cat sat down nearby. After she ordered a salad and the traditional ouzo, she thumbed through a small tour book.

The ouzo came right away. As always in Greece, the clear, strong liquid with the hearty anise flavor was served alongside a large glass of cold water. Cat poured the ouzo into the water and stirred it.

"Ah, I see you know how to drink ouzo correctly on a hot summer afternoon. Many Americans try to drink the ouzo and then hurry to wash it down afterward with the water."

Cat looked across at the gentleman who had addressed her from the nearby table. He was not as old she had thought initially. No more than in his late thirties, she decided. He was darkly handsome, with finely chiseled features in a thin, angular face. In fact, he reminded her a lot of Luke. She felt a flash of loneliness as she smiled across at him. "It's more refreshing this way—and it goes down a lot easier." She took a long sip. "Are you Greek?"

"I am as Greek as you are American—correct?" He had a charming smile.

"Correct. Unfortunately, my mastery of the Greek language is nonexistent. How did you learn to speak English so well?"

"May I join you at your table and explain?"

Cat nodded a little hesitantly. She hoped the man did not assume she was interested in being picked up. It just seemed pleasant to have a nice chat over lunch before she headed over to the Acropolis.

"Allow me to introduce myself. I am Nikolas Panos, assistant curator of the Folk-Art Museum. Have you ever been there?"

"No. But it sounds interesting."

"You must come—as my guest. Besides the wonderful embroidery—sad to say, almost a dying art now—we have the finest collection in Greece of Theophilos Hadjimichael's artwork."

"Well, then I must come. I'm sorry to say I've never even heard of this artist, but from the way you say his name, he must be very special."

Nikolas Panos nodded serenely. "Tomorrow, if you come in the morning, I will be free to show you around. I assume this afternoon you are heading for the Acropolis."

"Yes. If I don't melt from the heat." She grinned.

"You do not look like the type." He gave her an assessing smile.

Cat had a strong feeling Nikolas Panos had every intention, after all, of picking her up. She was no longer so certain she was opposed to the notion. It might help settle in her own mind exactly how serious she was about pursuing her relationship with Luke.

Cat finished her salad and ouzo, agreeing to let Nikolas be her informal guide for the afternoon. She was glad she had already made plans with Joanie for tonight, not wanting to lock herself into a long evening with Nikolas as well, when she wasn't even sure she was doing something sensible.

They stepped out of the restaurant into the middle of the Agora, the ancient remnants of a once flourishing marketplace.

Nikolas began his tour by pointing out the Stoa of Attalus. "This beautiful reconstruction," he explained, "was built in 1956 for people to have the experience of what a second-century indoor shopping center was like."

They walked inside. Cat had passed by several times in the past, never pausing to visit the reconstruction. Now she realized what she had missed. On the outside, the structure, with its uniform rows of Doric and Ionic columns, gave no hint of the lovely interplay of light and shadow within.

"It's beautiful. If I close my eyes I can see the people donned in togas browsing about, looking for bargains," she added with an impish grin.

Nikolas chuckled. "I'm sure they found some. But these market places weren't only for commerce. They existed in every large city and were used for public meetings and just hanging out."

"Watching all the girls go by?"

"But, of course. We Greeks have always appreciated a beautiful woman. I am no exception." He gave her a more intimate appraisal as he smiled warmly.

Cat began to regret her decision. His interest seemed only to spark memories of another outing— that one in Ghirardelli Square in San Francisco. She suggested they head on to the Acropolis.

They strolled leisurely up toward the west side of the Acropolis, following the ancient Panathenaic

Way. As they entered the Parthenon, Cat commented on its lovely salmon-colored marble.

"It was once sparkling white, as were all the buildings up here. This beautiful tint you see is the product of modern pollution."

"It touches everything, doesn't it?"

He smiled wistfully, his hand reaching out for hers. "Shall we walk?"

He guided her toward the south slope past Niki Apteros, a temple dedicated to the Athenian victories over the Persians. Only eighteen feet by twelve feet, this miniature building was a perfect gem. A few steps south, Cat came to an abrupt stop, gazing down at Herodes Atticus' theater. It was a spectular sight, a theater that was built in the second century A.D. and was still used for performances today.

"Now I'm in my element," Cat said with a grin.

"An actress. I should have known."

Cat corrected his impression. Although Nikolas was well-versed in the English language, she had a hard time explaining the nature of her work. Even when he finally understood, he looked quite skeptical.

They sat down on the stone steps of the theater. Cat stared across at the exquisite facade that framed the stage. Her eyes focused on the ancient stone, but her mind wandered back to Luke. She remembered how he, too, had first thought she was an actress. She wondered what he was doing right now.

"You are a woman in love, yes?"

"What? No. I mean . . . Why do you ask me that question?"

"You keep drifting off, and there is a special look in your eyes when you do. You are far too beautiful to be without a lover. A pity for me," he said wistfully. "I knew when I saw you in the taverna that you must be in love. He is someone very special, then. And very lucky."

"Nikolas, you are so Greek. All Greeks are romantics, are they not?" she grinned.

"Yes. Of course we are. In these surroundings," he said with a sweeping gesture, "how could we not be?" He took her hand again.

"I don't know if I'm in love. I don't think I can be. There hasn't been enough time. The trouble is, I'm not sure I ought to give myself the time to find out if it *could* become love."

"You will," he said with confidence.

"A soothsayer, too."

"No. Just a man who has had some modest experience with women and knows when they will follow a chosen course. I feel certain, in your heart, that you have made your decision to seek out your man."

"I think, Nikolas Panos, that you are a perceptive and kind man. Thank you for this afternoon. You may not realize how valuable it has been for me."

"Ah, I think that means I will not see you tomorrow at my museum."

"Tomorrow I will be taking a ferry to Skiathos."

"Skiathos. A most beautiful island. An island made for love."

When Cat returned to the hotel, she found a note from Joanie saying that there would be one more person joining them for dinner, and could she meet them at the Vassilis nearby.

Cat showered, changed into a cool, silk lilac dress, and walked over to the restaurant. Joanie was already seated at a table nursing an ouzo. Sitting beside her, sipping a beer, was Dodger. Both of them looked up awkwardly as Cat joined them.

"What have we here? A truce?" Cat asked cheerfully in an attempt to ease the tension.

"Just barely," Joanie muttered.

"This was a stupid idea," Dodger said at the same time.

Joanie narrowed her gaze at Dodger, then she looked over at Cat. "I love this man, Cat. Why, I don't know. He's stubborn, foolish, irascible. . . ."

Cat, a little taken aback by Joanie's forthright statement, had to catch her breath before responding. "I'm his daughter," Cat said, her turn to feel awkward. "I know those traits better than most people." She wasn't sure whether to include Joanie in that group.

"That's why I insisted he join us. I haven't been able to talk any sense into him. Maybe you can."

"Joanie," Dodger said, irritated, "we've been through this a hundred times. I'm not taking the best years of your life away."

"There he goes again." She focused on Cat, who was still not sure just what the fight was all about. "I'm thirty-three years old, Cat. I grant you, I'm not ready for the rocking chair, but I'm not some flighty young thing who is just starting to live and has no idea what she wants. I've had—experiences. Dodger and I have been through all that. He thinks because he's a little older that me—"

"Twenty years is no little bit older," he told her.

Ignoring him, Joanie went on. "He feels he's robbing the cradle. I think he's scared that's what others would think, you especially."

Cat swallowed hard. It was what she *had* thought —exactly. But looking at the two of them now, she could sense that beneath the arguing and grumbling, Dodger and Joanie were in love with each other.

To confirm it, she asked, "Do you love her, Dodger?"

He started to buck, then sighed. "Love isn't always enough, Cat. I've learned that from experience."

"You didn't answer me, Dad."

He looked from Cat to Joanie. "I love her. I love her so much, I'm not going to ruin her life by roping her to a man whose own life is more than half over."

"It seems to me that what's ruining Joanie's life is all the wasted time she's spending pining away for you. Look, it isn't for me to tell you two what to do, but if you're worried about my reaction, don't be. Sure, I'll admit at first it felt a little strange to see the two of you together. But not

184

anymore. Now—now it just seems right." She fought back tears. Although her sudden desire to cry had nothing to do with Joanie and Dodger, she knew that they would automatically assume it did.

Tomorrow couldn't come fast enough.

Luke combed the beach for seashells. He had amassed quite an interesting collection during his two weeks on Skiathos. His promised week off before he buckled down to his book had stretched into two. He felt no more ready today than fourteen days ago to write about sexual fulfillment. Beyond gathering shells, all he'd been able to do for the last few weeks was to *think* about sexual fulfillment—that and a dozen other aspects of fulfillment that all revolved around Cat Roy.

She was constantly on his mind. Every day, on the beach, sight-seeing in the towns, sitting in cafés, he would imagine he saw her whenever a tall, thin, dark-haired woman walked by. The disappointment each time in seeing some sadly lacking look-alike invariably ruined the rest of his day.

He picked up a shimmering piece of coral and tossed it over to his pile. A young woman in a scant bikini was just passing his blanket as he threw it. It grazed her shoulder, and she let out a surprised cry.

"I'm terribly sorry." Luke rushed over.

"It's nothing," she said. "I was more startled than hurt." She bent to pick up the coral and tossed it with better aim toward his other shells and stones. "Quite a collection. Is it your hobby?"

Luke smiled. "It's starting to feel that way."

"Bloody hot today," she commented, sweeping her long blond hair off her shoulders. "Are you here on holiday from the States?" she asked pleasantly.

"Part holiday. What about you?"

"I'm working as a waitress over at the Nostos Hotel for the summer, and then it's back to London in the fall. I'm a schoolteacher when I'm not bumming about on summer holidays, which, unfortunately, I have to combine with some work in order to play. Actually, the Nostos is a marvelous hotel—very posh, you know—and the tips are very good. There now, I've told you my story. Except my name. Glenna Mitchell." She extended a slender, well-tanned arm.

As they shook hands, Luke observed that Glenna was not only a loquacious young woman, but also a very attractive one with her golden blond hair cascading over her shoulders, jade-green eyes that blatantly checked him out, and a voluptuous body that more than did justice to what there was of her bathing suit.

He was also well-aware that he was being picked up by this gorgeous creature. The realization caused him a mixture of discomfort and curiosity. Glenna might be just the remedy for what was ailing him. Of course, the minute he thought of remedies, he thought of Cat and her secret brews. His tentative interest in Glenna Mitchell was lost to his memories of other days.

Glenna noticed the sudden change in Luke's

interest as he introduced himself, but today was her day off and she was not in the mood to spend it alone. Not that she couldn't have started a mild flirtation with any number of men on the beach that day, but Luke particularly attracted her. Maybe what appealed to her was the fact that he lacked that lecherous leer she so often saw in men's eyes. Whatever, she decided to put forth some more effort. She started by asking if she could join him, and when he nodded hesitantly, she sat down on his blanket, idly looking through his shells.

"So tell me about the other part of your visit to Greece," she said lightly.

He looked at Glenna, a small smile on his lips. He remembered Cat's amused grin when he'd told her about his book. To the young, attractive woman next to him he merely said, "I'm working on a psychiatry textbook. Very dull and tedious, which is why I'm out here on the beach this morning instead of behind my typewriter."

She gave him a sympathetic smile. "Reminds me of the boredom of doing school papers. At least I've a few months' reprieve from that." She stretched out on her back. Luke took a quick glance at her tanned body sprawled out beside him and hastily looked out to sea. He might not be interested in getting involved with the woman beside him, but he was not fool enough to think her appearance would leave him blank.

He excused himself to go for a swim. Glenna tagged along, joining him back on the blanket afterward. Luke reached for his watch.

"Look, pal," Glenna said as Luke began wrapping his shells inside a T-shirt, "you seem to have a lot on your mind. I get the picture that you're not desperate to sweep me off my feet, but it is a beautiful day, which I do have off from the hotel. I like you. Maybe we could just spend a few hours together—go see some sights, have some lunch. . . ."

He started to turn down her offer, but there was such a warm, friendly smile on her face that he found himself saying yes. After all, he was lonely as well; the sun was getting too strong to spend more time at the beach, and yet, he did not want to go back to his bungalow to work; and Glenna was chatty, pleasant, and easy on the eye.

They decided to take the ferry over to Alonnisos, another small island in the area. Luke had not been there, and Glenna recommended it highly as one of the less touristed islands still retaining the flavor of old Greece.

Luke's spirits started out high enough, but as the day wore on, he kept finding things that Glenna said or did that reminded him of Cat. They took a speedboat ride, and he thought about the cruise around San Francisco; they wandered around the small marketplace and he remembered Ghirardelli; they stopped for ices at a local seaside stand, and he could see Cat stretched out on her hotel room bed, asking him to order up pistachio ice cream from room service.

When he dropped Glenna off at her hotel, neither of them made any mention of getting together again. It had turned out to be a disappointing outing for both of them. Luke, tense and lonelier than this morning, stopped at a local taverna for an ouzo.

A few hours later, much the worse for wear after several more ouzos than he should have drunk, he stumbled back to his bungalow to sleep it off.

He was quite aware he'd overdone the ouzo, but he didn't think he was really drunk. Until he stepped inside his small cottage and discovered he was beginning to hallucinate.

Stretched out on his bed was a vision of Cat, as real as life, looking more exquisite than the past few weeks of his fantasies and memories combined. It was then that he was certain, beyond a shadow of a doubt, that he was utterly, completely intoxicated.

CHAPTER ELEVEN

When Luke woke up the next morning, he was aware of only two things—the worst hangover he'd ever experienced and the memory of the most vivid sensual dream he could ever recall. He sat up, looking over to the other side of the bed, not really surprised to find it empty, yet still feeling a sharp twinge of disappointment.

They had made love with such a passionate intensity. Cat had never looked more beautiful, nor ever felt more exquisite. Her touch had seared every part of his body with desire. He had held her to him with possessive demand. And she had given herself with utter abandon, her slender, agile body a wonder of grace and movement. They had each surrendered fully to a need that was beginning to turn into an obsession.

The dream had been too vivid, too real. Luke's

pounding head seemed mild compared to the pain in his heart. He ran his fingers through his tangled hair and moaned softly.

"I bet you've got yourself quite a swelled head this morning, Dr. Eliot."

His eyes sprang open, mouth dropping in stunned amazement. For a brief moment he thought he could be having another hallucination.

"You've got that look in your eye again, Doc." Cat laughed. "Here, drink this." She handed him a bright red concoction in a tall glass.

Luke took it out of her hands, set it on the table, and then grabbed her. She fell on top of him on the bed.

"I'm real, all right," she whispered. "You don't have to break some bones to prove it."

She kissed him then. "This wasn't the cure I had in mind," she murmured as he grasped her more tightly, kissing her back.

"You are real." He stared intently into her eyes, sparkling sea-blue in the morning sun. "What are you doing here?"

"Aren't you glad to see me?" she teased. "You certainly seemed pretty happy last night."

"My God, last night! It wasn't a dream."

"Most definitely not. You're something else when you've been nipping at the ouzo."

"What do you mean? I didn't hurt you, did I?"

Cat laughed. "Let's just say that when you inadvertently did, you made up for it with flying colors. Not that I recommend we make love under those conditions regularly. I prefer romantic afterglow to your passing out cold."

Luke still looked stunned, but he was trying to take it all in.

She placed a cool hand on his brow. "Lay down, Doctor. You need some rest. I do seem to get to play Florence Nightingale a lot when I'm with you. We're just going to have to see to it that you start taking better care of yourself from here on out." She gently shoved him back on the pillow, but Luke was not about to let her out of his grasp. She came willingly, nestling against his chest.

"I missed you, Luke. God, I missed you." Her throaty voice trembled with feeling.

He hugged her tightly. "I missed you, too."

"I know. You told me so last night. You told me quite a lot of things last night," she said, seductively placing a moist kiss on the palm of his hand.

Luke stirred, sitting up slightly, his elbows digging into the mattress for support. "What exactly did I say?"

She gave him a mischievous smile. "Don't you remember?"

He grinned back. "You devil." He grabbed her, but she put her hands on his chest, pushing against him so that he fell back on the pillow.

"Whatever I did say last night," he said with renewed passion as she slid on top of him, "I meant it."

He kissed her eyelids closed, then traced the delicate shape of her face with his lips. He followed the line of her chin to her throat, edging her over on her back, so that he could continue his languid, sensuous exploration.

Cat could feel her body yielding easily as she curved into his caresses, her senses absorbed by his touch and the feel of him. As he teasingly stroked her flat belly with his tongue, she arched her back, her flesh tingling, trembling. Her hands reached out for him. He caught hold of her wrists.

He smiled at her as she opened her eyes. "Lie still for a while and just let me give you pleasure. I missed a hell of a lot last night, and I want to make up for it this morning."

He kissed each of her fingertips and then placed her hands in a sensuous pose above her head. After a look of approval, he slid his hands to her breasts, cupping them lovingly, tasting the taut, sweet nipples, then gazing up at her as Cat's eyelids flickered closed, her lips parting slightly.

He moved slowly along her body, brushing light, tender kisses on her skin, tanned more now than a few weeks ago. His hands took possession of her hips as he drank in her wild-flower fragrance.

Cat cried out in pleasure as his touches grew more erotic, his lips more intimate. She began to move in a sensuous, undulating motion as Luke intensified his own movements. Finally, poised on a precipice of throbbing desire, she thrust her fingers into his thick, tangled hair, her body arched against him. He slid up to meet her lips, their kiss hungry, urgent. When at last he filled her, she circled her legs tightly around his thighs, letting herself go completely, drowning in glorious waves of pleasure, shuddering deeply as the sheer power of the moment culminated in sweet ecstasy.

Later, after Luke had more than made up for his passing out last night, he asked her again what she was doing in Greece.

When she told him about the film, he wasn't surprised. However, he was disappointed. It would have fit his own fantasy better had she simply come after him with no other motivation than a driving need to be with him. Now he had to share her with her work, worrying constantly about her luck running out one of these days when she took a leap off some building.

"You look unhappy," she observed. "I could have taken a job in Mexico. I chose this one because I've known since our last time in San Francisco that I wasn't going to be able to forget you. Now I'm convinced of it."

She slid out of the bed, gathering her scattered clothes up from the floor. "I shouldn't have bothered dressing this morning. How foolish of me to think one little hangover would stop a man of your remarkable stamina." She winked slyly and then proceeded to get dressed again.

"Why the rush to get dressed?"

"I'm supposed to dive off a cliff in Alonnisos at two. If we hurry, we'll make the noon ferry."

"We?"

Cat came over and sat down on the bed beside Luke as she ran a brush through her hair. "Come with me, Luke. If we're going to be involved with each other, you're going to have to get used to what I do to put bread on my table."

"I can think of a million safer ways to buy bread," Luke said, his tone sulky.

"Luke, that's the reason I want you to come along and watch. You have the wrong idea about stunting. I never do anything that is too great a risk. If you really look with your eyes and not your runaway imagination, you'll realize every stunt is carefully controlled and monitored."

"So tell me why so many people in your business have wound up in hospitals—and funeral homes. I did some reading after you were gone. There are quite a few books on your line of work, but to be perfectly honest, after I read the statistics on injuries and fatalities in the first book, I felt too ill to read any further."

Cat was silent for a minute. Then she looked across at Luke and sighed. "I'm not going to argue the point. I'm sure the book recorded accurate statistics, but I'm not a statistic, Luke. I enjoy life too much to go taking dumb chances. You're concentrating on the few crazy daredevils who took foolish risks rather than on professional stunters like me. You've checked me out enough times, now," she said in a low, seductive voice. "See any scars—or even a large scratch?"

He did know every inch of her body and there wasn't a scratch, large or small, on her.

"Get dressed and come with me. I promise you'll feel less worried if you watch the precautions I take. I was asked to do this stunt today, for instance, wearing a bikini, but I insisted on a full, one-piece tank suit with lots of padding, so I didn't damage those parts of me I know you love so well."

Her seductive banter was having its desired effect. Luke drew her to him for a long, deep kiss.

"You win." He sighed, reaching for the glass Cat had offered him earlier. He drank it all down. "Something tells me that my headache could return."

Cat turned out to be half-right, half-wrong in her estimation of how Luke would feel when he watched her execute her stunt dive. As he followed her climb up the steep cliff, a sinking feeling took complete control of his stomach. Yes, she wore that padded suit she told him about, even though he overheard the director arguing with Dodger about the bikini up to the last minute. Yes, she had first checked out the water with several other crew members to make sure there were no hidden rocks below the surface. And yes, she showed every caution as she executed a perfect test dive off one of the smaller cliffs.

Still, when he watched her arch her body for that final dive, he felt a riveting fear. Even when she surfaced from the water, waving and bright-eyed from the thrill and the excitement, his heart was still pounding a mile a minute. He could not deny that she was wonderfully talented, but he still couldn't shake the fears inside him that her work generated.

To make matters worse, Dodger and Cat had a rousing fight shortly after Cat stepped out of the dressing room. Although Luke was too far away to hear the specifics, he picked up enough to know it had to do with some upcoming stunts Cat was planning on.

"Let's get something cold to drink," she said to Luke after leaving Dodger in a huff.

"Am I going to meet your father one of these days?"

"Tonight. Right now he's in a lousy mood."

She took a firm hold of his hand. "Come on. There's a taverna I spotted on our way over here. It's just around the bend."

Luke stuck with lemonade. Cat ordered ouzo.

"You don't look too cheerful, yourself," Luke said lightly, trying to push aside the tension still clinging to him from her dive.

Shrugging off his comment, she said, "Wasn't that a neat little stunt today? My next one is going to really be sweet."

"Oh," he said distractedly, hoping she wouldn't give him the details. His stomach was just beginning to settle down.

"It's a standard stunt, really," she said, oblivious to his wishes, "but I've added a few little touches to spark some more life into it."

"Are those the sparks that caused the fight with your father before?"

"Dodger?" She groaned. "He is impossible sometimes. I have to try to stop letting him get

197

me all riled up. I know what I'm doing, and if he doesn't—well, that's tough. Look, it's simple. . . ."

"Cat, do me a favor and spare me the details. For one thing, I probably won't understand them any more than you would follow my treatise on Winnicott's theories on maturational processes in a facilitating environment."

"That's a mouthful," she said sarcastically. "And what's the second reason?"

"The second reason is that your feats of derring-do continue to terrify me. I still think you're in a business that will ultimately end up with you getting hurt. I get especially tense about this whole thing when I overhear your father telling you he thinks the little extra sparks you're adding to the stunt—excuse me, gag—are too dangerous."

"Well, at least you are picking up the lingo." She had to smile. "Listen to me, Luke. I know I tend to push myself to my outermost limits. I'm a perfectionist. Don't you see, that's what keeps me safe. My father gets carried away at times with being overly cautious because I'm his one and only daughter. Keep in mind, Luke, that Dodger's my one and only dad. I don't need two fathers, believe me."

Cat took a long sip of her ouzo and water and went on. "Maybe you're right. I would think you were talking Greek if you spouted some deep psychiatric jargon, and you feel the same about my profession. So why can't we just respect what the other person is doing and assume we can handle our own professions without interference? How would you like me telling you how to deal with a mentally disturbed patient?"

"You present a good argument. Ever think of switching to law?"

Cat sighed. "You're hopeless, Doc. I'm going to have to get you drunk on ouzo again tonight. You have a much more interesting spiel when you're tipsy."

"You never did tell me what I talked about in my weakened condition last night." He grinned at her broadly.

She leaned close to him, her breasts crushed against his arm. "Did you really almost go mad with longing for me all those weeks; your dreams each night filled with erotic fantasies? Shall I remind you of some of the details of those dreams?"

"Later," he whispered. "What do you say we get out of here?"

When Cat introduced Luke to Dodger that night at the hotel dining room, the two men sized each other up after shaking hands. On close inspection Luke could see a clear resemblance between father and daughter. He could also tell by the way Dodger studied him that he had not known much, if anything, about Luke's involvement with his daughter, and he was clearly puzzled by it.

Luke's assessment was right on target. Dodger saw Luke Eliot as the most unlikely man he would have ever imagined his daughter getting involved with. On the other hand, he wasn't a stunter, so he already had one large point in his favor as far as Dodger was concerned.

"So what do you think of that stunt Cat pulled off today? I spotted you on the side watching. Wasn't sure then . . . uh, what your connection was to Cat, else I would have come over and introduced myself."

"I thought she was spectacular and she scared the . . . pants off of me. Maybe you get used to it in time," Luke said honestly.

Dodger laughed, giving Luke a friendly pat on the back. "I still feel a knot in the pit of my stomach every time she goes out in front of a camera. And when she was a kid—let me tell you, my friend, she scared . . . the pants . . . off me every other minute with her wild pranks. She's a terror, this little girl of mine. Headstrong, restless . . . I won't say crazy, seeing as how that's your profession and you'll have to be the judge on that one. But, she's probably the best female stunter in the business. Best there ever was." He put his arm around Cat in an affectionate squeeze.

"I don't know if you're going to scare Luke off more because of my impossible qualities or my shining talents." Cat only half-teased. "Luke and I don't see eye to eye on my profession."

"You've got my vote, Luke," Dodger said. "As good as she is, I rather see her home knitting booties any day."

Cat flushed. She was angling to keep her relationship with Luke afloat, not sink it into wedlock, and Luke felt the same way. He was barely getting adjusted to Cat being back in his life. He was certainly nowhere near the wedding bells stage.

"Stop looking like I just told you both the world was coming to an end. Just making general talk. Well, actually, not so general. Where the hell is she, anyway?" he grumbled, checking his watch. "That woman is going to have to learn to be a little quicker after we get hitched."

"Hitched?"

"Oh, damn it. Now I've gone and done it. Joanie will have a fit. We were supposed to break the news together. There she is. Shush. Pretend I didn't say a word."

Joanie rushed over to their table. "Not my fault," she said breathlessly. "Thank our dear director for calling a six o'clock meeting to go over tomorrow's effects." She sat down and smiled at Luke as Cat introduced them.

Since the others had already made their choices, Joanie scanned the menu quickly. As she did so, there was dead silence. Joanie looked up. First she eyed Dodger, then Luke, then Cat.

"He already told you, didn't he?" She gave Dodger a sly look.

"It slipped out." He smiled sheepishly.

Cat could not remember another time in her whole life that Dodger had worn a sheepish grin. Joanie was bringing out qualities in her dad she had not known existed.

Joanie grinned, then leaned over and kissed him, ruffling his hair in the process. "I finally won an argument with this stubborn old fool."

"See, already you're calling me old," Dodger said, but there was only warm teasing in his tone.

"I'd call you a few other things, if Cat and Luke weren't around," Joanie teased back.

"Hey"—Cat grinned—"we're family, at least I am," she quickly amended. She did not want to inadvertently lead Dodger into talk about a possible double wedding. "Feel free to give Dodger a piece of your mind anytime you like."

"Maybe I ought to back out," Dodger said, sighing. "Now I'm going to have two women always on my back."

"Too late. She could sue you for breach of promise," Cat said, poking him in the shoulder.

After they gave their orders, Joanie's expression grew serious.

"How do you feel about Dodger and me, Cat? I mean, you and your dad have been teamed up for a long time. . . ."

Cat reached out for Joanie's hand. "I think you are the best thing that's ever happened to Dodger." She glanced over to her father and back again to Joanie. "Besides, it's about time he settled down, instead of bugging me to do it all the time."

"I'm setting a precedent that those who come after me can follow," Dodger butted in. "What do you think, Luke?"

Luke muttered something incoherent but was saved from repeating it as the salads arrived just then.

A couple of hours later, Cat and Luke walked together down to the ferry. It was the last one back to Skiathos, and he did not intend to miss it. Cat was not planning to join him.

"You were quiet tonight. Silent, as a matter of fact." Cat stared straight ahead as they walked.

"I was the outsider at a family celebration. I guess there wasn't much for me to talk about."

"I'm surprised Joanie is going to quit the business. Not that being an assistant special effects person is the kind of career someone would want for the rest of their lives. Still, I can't understand her wanting to sit quietly at home darning Dodger's socks as they grow quietly old together."

"You plan to jump out of windows until you're old and gray?"

"I don't plan to sit in a little white cottage with a picket fence baking pies and cookies while I'm still young and able."

"I guess I don't see you baking cookies, anyway."

They walked in silence for a while.

"How's your book coming?"

"Terribly. I'm a week behind schedule already. If I don't buckle down I'm going to start feeling a little guilty about all this sun and fun."

Cat gave him a curious glance. "I guess this trip can't be all fun and games for either of us. We both have our work to do."

"Right."

They saw the ferry pulling into the dock.

Luke grabbed Cat's arm so abruptly, she almost lost her balance and fell against him in the process.

"Listen to me, Cat. I don't want this fantasy to

end. But I can't quite deal with it moving along at fast speed. Let's just slow it down a little, okay?"

"It's going too fast for me, too, Luke. Why don't we cool off for a few days? I don't have to be on the set on Friday. If you've caught up enough on your work, come over to my bungalow. It has a little kitchenette. I may not be the pastry and pie type, but I have cooked a great dinner on occasion." She cocked her head, her eyes sparkling with that touch of mischief never far from view. "I might even make some instant chocolate pudding for dessert. See, I do have a domestic side to my nature."

"Great." He bent down to kiss her good-bye. "I'll bring over some of my torn socks, then."

He reached the ferry just before it began to pull out. After he stepped over the low-slung chain, he turned back to wave to Cat. She looked so beautiful as she stood on the dock, the wind blowing her dark hair, a gentle smile on her lips. He wished he hadn't said that good-bye. He never had gotten to hear the details of what he'd told her the night before. He wanted to hold on to the fantasy—to the magic they created when they were together.

Cat watched the ferry drift out to sea. She remained long after it disappeared over the horizon. She wished she had been as daring tonight as she'd been while doing her stunt today.

As soon as he had kissed her good-bye and headed toward that ferry, she knew she wanted to be with him. Sure, she was scared. So was Luke.

But as soon as the vision of being in his warm embrace surfaced, all those fears seemed to evaporate. She finally turned away and walked back toward her empty bungalow. Sometimes, she decided, she calculated the odds too carefully.

CHAPTER TWELVE

"It's burned."

"No, it isn't. A bit charred, that's all. I like it that way."

"Don't be ridiculous, Luke. You aren't going to hurt my feelings. I told you domesticity wasn't my thing. This proves it." Cat stared at his burned steak.

"You didn't have to prove it," he said, grinning.

"What's that supposed to mean? No, don't tell me. Despite my layman's understanding of your profession, I know you think I burned your steak on purpose."

"Did you?"

"Of course not. I wanted to make that steak for you. I don't eat meat, but I can cook it. Maybe my mind was on other things."

"Some stunt you're doing tomorrow?" There was a bite to his words.

"No." She shot him a cool glance, then lowered her eyes.

This night was not going according to plan for either of them. Apart all week, they had both indulged in fantasy, dreaming of being together again and regretting the wait they had imposed on themselves.

Luke had been able to work on his book mainly out of a need to keep his mind off Cat. He had skipped his proposed plan to work afternoons only, using mornings and evenings to relax. There was no relaxing without Cat. So he'd worked ten, sometimes fifteen hours a day, hoping at night to be so exhausted he would collapse into sleep. Most nights, that didn't work.

As soon as he let his guard down, Cat popped right into his mind. While at times the images were sensuous and pleasurable, more often than not, serious concerns kept crowding out the pleasant fantasies. It was one thing, he realized, to slip away from reality into a unique relationship for a brief while. But he and Cat had moved beyond the fantasy when she showed up in his bungalow and they both realized they could not end what they had begun.

The days without Luke were hectic ones for Cat. She did not have to call forth any self-imposed concentration to keep her mind on her work. The stunts for this film were more numerous and riskier than any she had ever done. She might deny it to Luke, but she and Dodger were well aware that Whitney's film was pushing her to her limits. For the most part, she felt confident about what he asked her to do, but a few times she joined Dodger in arguing against a particular stunt operation.

At night, she returned to her bungalow drained and exhausted. The problem was, when she slid under the covers of her bed, all she wanted was to have Luke's loving arms around her, to feel safe and secure in what was becoming a stable anchor in her life.

That was what scared her the most. Stability had never been something she searched out or wanted. Even now, its comfort made her uneasy. She sometimes felt like it was a rope being tied around her. Only, she was the one doing the tying.

She laid some of the blame on her father's impending marriage to Joanie. Who wouldn't experience some envy at the loving, caring picture the two of them created together? Sure, there was a part of her that wondered what it would be like to have that kind of relationship. But there was another part of her that rebelled at the very thought of such a binding commitment.

She was completely unaware, as she sat across the table from Luke, that tears were rolling down her cheeks. Luke knelt down beside her. She opened her eyes as he brushed the tears away.

"Don't cry, Kitten," he whispered tenderly.

The sound of his loving voice made her cry more. Luke stood up and took her hand, leading her over to the couch. He sat her down, sitting beside her, taking her in his arms. He pressed his lips against her shimmering, silky-soft hair. A new feeling was stirring inside him. All this time, he had sensed the hidden vulnerability within Cat, but this was the first time she had really let it surface. Holding her against him, he felt a special loving warmth, a deep, protective caring for this woman who was usually so independent, so determined to be a free, untamed spirit.

"It isn't working out the way I planned," she murmured into the crook of his neck when the tears finally subsided. "I don't usually burn dinner, and I can't remember the last time I broke down and cried like this. And—and . . . Oh Luke, in my dreams everything goes so smoothly. I never wanted any man the way I want you. I've never felt this way before." She looked up at him, a tiny smile on her lips, her eyes a warm teal blue. "Do you think it's love?"

He put his arms around her and kissed her gently on the lips. Cat slipped her hands around his neck and kissed him back—a dozen tiny kisses on his lips, his eyelids, his neck, and back again to his lips.

"You see what I mean. I want you so badly, Luke. When I'm wrapped around you like this, everything but desire floats away like meaningless puffs of smoke."

Luke wanted nothing more than to make love to her right then. He wanted to let go of everything but his need for her. But he couldn't. There were too many unspoken issues that had been slowly but surely causing walls to be built between them.

He held her at arm's length. "Where there's smoke there's usually fire, Cat. That fire, once it starts, can destroy everything in its wake. I don't want that to happen to us."

Cat stared at him soberly, the desire in her eyes fading away as Luke's words penetrated.

"I'm scared, Luke. I'm scared that the fire has been smoldering right from that first moment we met. A moment out of time and place. That's how it felt to me. You appeared like magic, taking me into another world, another life."

Her eyes met his. "Everything about you makes me want you, Luke—and yet, strangely keeps me distant. Sometimes I try to imagine going off with you to one of your medical conferences. Remember that afternoon you flew out of the hotel to meet Teri? God, I was jealous."

Her voice grew softer. "I didn't even realize how jealous until the dreams began. Dreams of me rushing off to meet you at one of your important conferences. I would be at your side while all your colleagues shook your hand respectfully, listened to all your erudite words of wisdom with awed looks in their eyes. You'd be standing up behind a podium presenting your research paper, and the applause would fill the room. And I'd feel so proud, Luke."

She paused for a moment. "Then the dream would turn into a nightmare. Some guy in a beard, looking very sage, would come over to me. In my dream I know he's talking English, but I can't follow one single word. I look over to you for help and you rush over. Only, when you explain what this man is saying, I don't understand you, either.

"Then someone looking very much like Teri strolls by. She gives this smug little laugh and explains to this man that I do stunts. He stares at me as though I have just landed in my spacecraft and then he gazes at you with this pathetic look of pity in his eyes."

"Sounds like a terrible dream," he murmured, stroking her cheek. "Not too different from some of mine. I don't have to be a psychiatrist to do dream interpretation on any of them."

"I know. How does the song go? 'Two different worlds . . .' They must have written that one with us in mind."

Luke held her against him, his fingers gently caressing her back. When he spoke, his voice was filled with tender warmth.

"Since the day we met, I have been completely infatuated with you. You've sparked feelings and responses in me I never knew existed. Talk about jealousy. All those times I assumed Dodger was some suave older lover of yours, I thought I would burst with outrage. I never felt jealous of any woman in my life before you popped into view on that damn ledge.

"For a man who has lived his entire life following self-prescribed rules of order, I suddenly found myself being governed a good deal of the time by my impulses. I'll admit, some of those impulses

211

threw me for a loop—scared the hell out of me. But—and here's the thing that makes it all so crazy—I've never felt this wonderful, this alive, this much in love in my life."

"Oh, Luke."

Passion overtook them even as they both sensed that something was coming to an end. Their admissions made the inevitability of their separation that much nearer. It was as though they needed to confess the truth, share the depth of their feelings, so that they would be able to part with honesty, leaving something real and vital to treasure.

But at that moment, as Luke took Cat in his arms and she curved into him so perfectly, they could respond only to the love and need they shared. One last time, they grasped the moment, daring tomorrow to touch them.

Making love together was never the same. Always some new element came into play—new feelings, new discoveries, new innovations in the art of lovemaking that neither of them had ever before experienced. They may have crossed worlds to come together, but in each other's arms they created a unique, splendorous world of their own creation. Tonight was no different, except that the new quality in their words and actions was one of love. A love that was bittersweet.

Tears mingled with sighs; whispered words of caring were tinged with sadness. Longing blended with fear. They clung to each other, desperate to stretch out the moment, wanting to shut out reality one last time.

They succeeded. Luke took possession of Cat's body and soul as he made love to her with the intensity of a man who had to claim her as his own. He plundered her slender form with searing kisses, crushed her to him so tightly she was left breathless. She kissed him back with a hungry demand, her hands tantalizing him as she left her mark on every inch of his body.

When he carried her over to the bed, a naked Greek goddess in his arms, she clung to him, kissing him all the while. Her fingers could feel the flexing of his muscles as he tightened his hold on her. She loved the ease with which he carried her. His lean build hid a sinewy strength and power always visible in their lovemaking but never so much as now.

The strength of his passion transported her into another universe. When he gently laid her on the bed, she caught hold of his wrists, tugging him down on top of her. Even that momentary separation had made her feel cold and lonely.

He could feel the beat of her heart as she pressed his head to her. Cat sighed as his hand cupped her breast. His probing tongue captured a sweet, hardened nipple. His mouth tasted the tender bud deeply, sensuously. He took nibbling bites that sent shivers through her.

She rubbed her chin against his dark, glistening hair, like a kitten might do. A kitten with the passion of a tigress, the independence of a cat.

Releasing her nipple, his mouth traveled to her breasts and then down her rib cage, his hands tightly pressed against her hips. He could feel the subtle movements in her body with each of his caresses, her own erotic strokes on his burning flesh growing fiercer, her sensuous undulations intensifying.

"I love you, Cat," he whispered as he entered her.

"I love you, too. I always will." Her words erupted in quick, breathy sounds as he took control of her body and she let herself be led again to ecstasy.

They lay together for a long while afterward without saying a word. A few times Luke thought Cat had fallen asleep, but when he stirred, she would kiss him lightly on his neck or cheek or chest. Then he would take her in his arms and plant tender kisses on her lips. Finally, as the night slipped into dawn, they fell asleep, Luke's arm curled protectively, lovingly around her shoulders.

She was already dressed, cowgirl fashion, when he opened his eyes the next morning. A bright sun was shining through the window.

"What time is it?"

"Almost eight."

"Are you working today?"

She nodded.

"Cat?" He paused, not sure what he wanted to say. "When are you leaving Greece?" Those weren't the words in his heart, but they were strongly on his mind.

"At the end of next week."

He nodded.

Cat started to spoon some instant coffee into two mugs. She stopped in motion, set the spoon down, and walked over to the bed.

Luke stretched out his hand, and she sat down beside him.

"I'm starting on a new film in a few weeks."

"You don't take much time off, do you?"

"In this business, if you take too much time off, they find somebody else. "

"Where will you go for this next movie?"

"New York, for part of it. And then overseas to Switzerland. It's a movie about a group of mountain climbers in the 1930s. One brave young woman and four men who scale the peaks together. I'm stunting for Stephanie Chasen. Did you ever hear of her?"

He was seeing icy precipices before his eyes and didn't hear Cat's question.

"Luke?"

He looked at her, the image not fading completely. His fingertips brushed her neck, a faint smile on his lips.

"You are my wild spirit. I suppose you have to scale mountains, dive off cliffs. But I want you to know one thing. Wherever you go, whatever you do, you have a part of my heart with you." His eyes were moist with tears as he whispered once again, "I love you."

His words triggered her own tears. "I'm not sure I . . ."

"We're just not ready, Cat. Neither of us can

bridge the gap right now. When we met, we were traveling on roads leading to destinations that we still need to get to. We took a very special and wondrous detour. But we have to get back on that road again. If there was any way in the world I could get you to hitch a ride with me to where I'm going, I would do it. And I know you feel the same."

"I guess we both want to be in the driver's seat. I do love you, Luke. There is no doubt in my mind about that. But I've never believed in hitching a ride."

"You'd better get going," Luke said softly.

She nodded but made no effort to move. Her body felt suddenly weighted down, immobile. He drew her to him.

Their kiss was sweetly tender and loving. And this time it truly tasted of good-bye.

CHAPTER THIRTEEN

The ancient ferry, laboring under the weight of the few cars and passengers, made its way into port. Cat had come to the tiny island of Skiros a day before most of the cast and crew to go over a couple of stunts with Dodger and two other stunt men.

Skiros, among the least accessible and least touristed of the Sporades island chain, also seemed to Cat to be one of the most beautiful. She hoped being here would lift her spirits. She focused her attention on the medieval castle silhouetted in the distance, hundreds of fig trees decorating the picturesque countryside.

Dodger came over and rested his hands lightly on Cat's shoulders as the cars began to pull off the ferry. Cat continued to stare out in front of her, but she placed her hands over her father's.

For the past few days Dodger had been worried about Cat. She looked tired and drawn; she avoided being with him, or anyone else, for that matter. When she was working, she was testy, argumentative, and distracted. He had a good idea about the cause of her miserable state, but every time he so much as breathed Luke Eliot's name, she flared up.

"Beautiful, isn't it, Dodger?"

"Real nice. Let's just hope the weather holds out. I'm looking forward to winding this thing up." He had his own personal reasons for not wanting any delay. He and Joanie were going to get married as soon as they got back to the States. Now that they had decided, neither of them wanted to wait any longer than they had to. But Dodger had another reason for wanting to get this picture wrapped. Cat.

Dodger was banking on a change of scene to get his daughter back into a healthy frame of mind. Her tension was also rubbing off on him. He did not relish the idea of these last few stunts. They had saved the toughest for the last. One in particular, a spectacular car chase around the island, Cat in the lead car, his other two stunters behind in their cars, culminating in a wild three-car collision, had him especially nervous. It would have made him uptight no matter what—these choreographed crashes could be tricky under the most controlled of circumstances—but Cat's mood escalated his worry.

"We're going to run through the markings nice

and easy today," Dodger said as they walked together off the ferry. "We'll all ride through the route together, and I'll go over some last-minute changes—very minor—so there should be no problem. Okay?"

"Sure. I have a few changes, too. Very minor," she added before Dodger balked.

"Just don't you forget I'm running the show. I have the last word on switches."

"Fine." She sped up her step. Dodger caught her by the arm.

"Hold on, now. Whitney made it clear to me, Cat, that he's already well over budget on this damn film. He doesn't want to drive up the cost even higher by having to reshoot stunts. Those three cars cost plenty, and we only want to go around once."

Cat didn't answer.

"Maybe you'd better tell me those changes right here and now," Dodger said.

"Can we get onto shore first—or do you want to take a round trip ride again?"

He kept a tight grip on her elbow as they stepped on shore. Waving to the other stunters, he shouted, "Meet us over in that café." He motioned in the direction of a small taverna a few yards off the dock.

"Dodger, please."

"Please, what? If you have some wild notions in your head about doing some extra fancy driving gag, I want to hear about it."

"Okay, you win," she relented. "Remember the

movie *Deathwatch*—that final chase scene? Frank Evans coordinated it; George Corey ran it through."

"I remember it," he said cautiously. It was one of the better planned stunt chases he'd seen, and he had respect for Evans's talents. However, he'd worked with Corey on a couple of pictures and found the man to be too reckless and hotheaded.

"Well, Corey did a super blowout and spin-off in that chase. Just at the turn when he gets his speed up and the other cars are still far enough back, he comes down on the shoulder of the road and throws the car sideways. Then he—"

"I know what he did. Corey was crazy. If he didn't break a half-dozen bones in that gag I'll eat my hat. Forget it, Cat. You stick to the spins and keep your damn car off the shoulder of the road or I'll see to it that you never work on another one of my pictures again. Do you hear me?"

"Dodger, listen. I know Corey ran into trouble. But I also know why. I've made some changes—"

"You aren't making any changes." He stormed off in the direction of the taverna. A few steps away he came to an abrupt stop. Looking back over his shoulder, he called, "You coming or are you taking the ferry back?"

Cat took a deep breath. There was no point arguing with her father. Anyway, she had other means of getting her way. She walked toward Dodger, and they continued together on to the taverna.

Although Cat was at her most cooperative all afternoon, Dodger had an uneasy feeling that something was up. She was too compliant, too relaxed. He planned to talk with Peter when they got back tonight to make sure Cat didn't try to get the director on her side.

They returned to Alonnisos around five. The ferry coming back had been late, supposedly a natural occurrence. No one on the islands seemed to be in much of a hurry. The slow, relaxed pace of their lives contrasted sharply to the pace driving Cat these past days.

She had spent the first day after that final good-bye with Luke fighting back tears whenever she wasn't in front of the camera. Sometimes she wasn't successful. Then she would slip off into the woods or back to her bungalow or into the ladies' room at the local taverna and let the tears pour out. She'd sit for a while, managing to pull herself together, regaining her equilibrium, before she returned to the set. She was sure people were aware something was going on, but she avoided everyone enough not to have to answer any questions.

Liz, more than the others, figured out the story. She also knew that the ending was a real tearjerker. Cat was sure Liz would lend a shoulder just as she had done for her, but her grief felt too private, too personal to share. So she cried alone, the tears having no effect on the pain of the separation.

And yet, as much as Luke, she had agreed there was no other way. Even when she felt her most miserable, she never once ran to a phone to call him. What would she say? Was she going to tell him she was packing her bags to move to San

Francisco so she could try her hand at cooking steaks again? He didn't want a wife any more than she was ready to deal with a husband. She hadn't even done particularly well dealing with him as her lover.

She was beginning to get the tears under control. Her battle with Dodger on Skiros had helped. Cat's mind was now busily plotting how to get around what she viewed as her father's overly cautious concerns.

That evening she had dinner with Joanie and Dodger. Cat was in better spirits, except for the sharp, painful ache she felt when the happy couple discussed their romantic honeymoon plans. Dodger was suspicious of the change, but he was relieved to see his daughter smile for the first time in days.

"We were going to stay in Greece," Joanie said, reaching for Dodger's hand, "get married here and then tour some of the other islands. But we decided on a good old-fashioned church wedding with all the trimmings. And then, Niagara Falls." She grinned at Dodger. "That was your father's idea. He said it was his secret fantasy."

Dodger flushed. "Come on, Joanie. You thought it was a real romantic idea."

"It is." She leaned over and kissed his cheek.

"Now the only thing I've got to do," Joanie said to Cat, "is figure out some way to get your father to slow down his pace so we can fix up that ranch of his."

"You're moving out to the ranch?" Cat asked in surprise. "That place is a total shambles."

"That's how I managed to buy it in the first place," Dodger reminded her. The ranch, as they called it, was a ten-acre spread in the San Joaquin Valley. There was a house and barn on the property, both of which were barely still standing. It had been advertised as one of those handyman specials. Handy*men* was more like it—a good dozen of them at least.

"You don't want to take Joanie out there. It would take you years to get the house into shape."

"We're not only planning to fix up the house," Joanie said enthusiastically. "We want to do a little farming, maybe raise some horses and cattle. It will be slow going, but we're both real excited about it."

Cat smiled wistfully. "So I see." It must be nice, she thought, to want the same things out of life that the man you love wants. She wondered if she could ever make the kind of transition Joanie and Dodger were going to make. They'd both spent a lot of years always on the go, traveling from one side of the earth to the other. Cat had been on those travels with both of them and knew that they had felt the same excitement and wanderlust that she still felt. But now they seemed able to let go of that part of their lives for something else—a life-style that would allow them to be together, not just physically but in spirit as well.

Dodger looked across at Cat. "That spread of mine has plenty of space on it for another house. If you ever settle down someday . . ."

"I don't think so, Dodger. I guess I'm just not the settlin' type."

She couldn't see herself on that ranch any more than she could see herself with Luke at those medical conventions she'd had all those nightmares about.

The time for fantasy was over. She had to recapture the spirit and excitement of her work. And she knew just the way to do that.

By nine o'clock the meal was over. Cat stretched and told the lovebirds she was going to turn in early. She had a feeling they planned to do the same and was certain they would not be disappointed by her departure.

Her bungalow was in a small beach complex where the cast and crew occupied their own digs or buddied up with two or three others. Peter Whitney had a choice cottage right at the ocean's edge, as did the two co-stars. Instead of turning east toward her own place, Cat headed straight ahead toward the sea.

She knocked on Peter Whitney's door. A familiar voice invited her in.

"Hi, Cat." Liz Fuller, decked out in a very alluring "at home" soft blue silk gown, greeted Cat with casual ease. Dreamy mood music played in the background, the lights dimmed low.

"Sorry, I didn't mean to intrude," Cat answered, a note of surprise in her tone. Wasn't it a week ago that Liz was dabbing cotton on her tearstained face because of Tony Vargos and Cat was desperately trying to console her?

"Close your mouth, sweetie." Liz chuckled. "Even on you, it's not your most becoming image."

Cat laughed, shaking her head. "You are a wonder, Liz. I gather . . ."

"You gather right." Liz gracefully rose from her half-reclined position on the couch. She walked over to the makeshift bar to pour herself another glass of champagne and one for Cat.

"Sit down and let your shock subside. I know what you're thinking. How could I have forgotten all about my heartfelt passion for Tony? And how could I replace him with Peter, who I've cursed from one continent to another?"

"Where is Peter?" Cat asked, not taking the offered seat. She assumed Liz would not be so chatty if he were about to pop out of the next room, but Cat was not in the mood for chats.

"He really is a charmer," Liz went on blithely. "Believe me, no one could be more surprised than me. On the set the man is a horrible tyrant. I still think he's audacious, impossible, and pigheaded. We share a lot in common"—she grinned—"on and off screen. He's gone for some more champagne and I think, roses. Or some kind of flowers. He has this desire to see me—"

"That's okay. You can leave it to my imagination," Cat said, starting toward the door. "I'll catch Peter in the morning."

"Hold on. You haven't touched your drink. Peter won't be back for a few minutes, so you don't have to race out."

Cat stood awkwardly near the door. She took a sip of her champagne.

"What happened to 'blood sisters'?" Liz asked after a few moments.

"I'm fine, Liz," Cat said softly. There was no point denying the implication of Liz's remark. "Hearts heal, right? You certainly know that . . . sorry. I didn't mean that the way I think it sounded. The truth is, I envy your recuperative powers. I'm more than ready to take lessons, sis," she said with an affectionate grin.

"My heart wasn't broken over Tony. Just my pride. I also wasn't in love with him. If I was really stuck on the guy, I would never have let him off the hook so easily. I've learned that in love and movies you have to fight tooth and nail to get what you want."

"Well, I've never been particularly good at hammering nails in straight. Now I'm trying to be very mature and philosophical about the whole experience."

"How are you at philosophy?" Liz queried, a small smile on her lips.

"Lousy. I'm flunking my course in psychiatry, too. I figure the safest thing to do is stick to stunting. I've discovered it's much less risky than being in love." Cat laughed softly, but there was no humor to the sound. She set her glass of champagne on a nearby table and started toward the door. The last thing she needed right now was to be the third wheel in another hot romance.

She was just about to reach for the doorknob

when the door swung open. Peter rushed in, a bottle of champagne in one arm and a huge bouquet of olive branches in the other. Not roses but creative and romantic nonetheless, Cat thought. She took another step toward the door, eager to get around the man bearing gifts.

Peter wouldn't hear of it. At least not until he found out the reason for Cat's surprise visit.

"No problem on Skiros today?" Always the director first. He laid his gear on a chair.

Cat grinned. "Not a problem. I have a terrific idea for improving the gag."

"Obviously, Dodger doesn't agree. He left me a note warning me you might drop by, and he wants me to veto whatever you have in mind."

Liz sidled up to Peter. She gave Cat a sly smile. "Dodger has a pretty good notion of what's in his daughter's best interest. He also doesn't like to be crossed. Peter knows that from experience, right, darling?"

Before Peter could answer, Cat broke in. "Look, I don't want to—to keep you, but it's a minor change that would make the stunt terrifically dramatic. Dodger never gave me a chance to prove it's as safe as crossing the street. This could be a topper to *Bullitt*. All it requires are a few engineering changes to alter the car's suspension so that when I round my last turn before bailing out, I lean onto the shoulder and ride it off on two wheels. If we make sure the balance is right, I come back down on all fours, take my spin and bail out as planned."

227

"You're crazy, Cat," Liz argued, concerned by the look of excitement on her friend's and her director's faces. "That car is rigged with enough dynamite to blow you to kingdom come if you misjudge a fraction and topple that Porsche instead of righting it. I may not do the stunts, but after all these years in the business, I know when a gag is insane."

"Dodger will never go along with it," was Peter's comment.

"I don't intend for him to know about it. You give me the okay, make sure the mechanics keep their mouths closed about the alterations to my car—and get ready to film the most spectacular car gag of your film career."

"Cat!" Liz pleaded, then turned to Peter. "She's going to get herself killed. You can't allow her to do it."

"Peter," Cat broke in, ignoring Liz, "it sounds like a reckless, daredevil piece of insanity, but believe me, I've worked it out to the letter. I can do it. I'm not looking for an early entry to heaven. I have no intention of even getting scratched on this ride. It will make this chase one of the best ever done."

"You're sure you can keep that baby under your control?"

Cat smiled. "You just watch me."

Liz knew she was not going to be able to talk sense into either of them. Certainly not Cat. Now that Cat had won Peter over, she had that look of determination in her eye that defied anyone to get in her way. Maybe later Peter would be more amenable to listening to reason.

Luke wasn't working on his book; he had no heart for wandering the beach collecting seashells; and he'd lost his taste for ouzo. Several times he thought seriously about packing up and heading for home. But something held him here. He was well aware that that "something" was Cat.

He had spent days telling himself everything had worked out for the best. Certainly, if this whole business had happened to one of his patients, he would have been completely supportive of the man's determination to break off a no-win situation. So why was he feeling so damn miserable?

Time, he told himself, was all he needed. You don't fall madly in love with someone and feel no pain after a few days—even when you know that ending it rationally is the sanest thing to do.

Max Hart sprang into his mind. What was it his friend had said? A little insanity is sometimes healthy. Luke had to admit one thing. Pure sanity could feel like hell.

The worst time for Luke was when he'd go out for the evening—take a long walk or sip beer in a local taverna—then return to his bungalow and look over at his empty bed. Maybe there was still a touch of madness left in him. He kept finding himself wishing for hallucinations, wanting visions of Cat to dance before his eyes, wanting to see her sensuous form sprawled out on his sheets.

No magical visions appeared, but memories continued to haunt him. And dreams. That morning he had woken up in a sweat. The same had happened for the past few days. He kept having sickening nightmares of Cat going through one of her stunts. Something would always go wrong. In his previous nightmares he could sense impending disaster, but he always managed to wake himself up before anything actually happened. That morning the horror of his awful dream had held him in its clutches to the bitter end. When he finally woke up, his sweat was accompanied by a trembling feeling in his body. He couldn't seem to shake the dream from his mind.

He got out of bed, made himself some breakfast, and ran down to the beach for a swim. When he got back to the bungalow, the local woman who came each morning to straighten up was already there. Luke's bathing suit was nearly dry, and he put off changing while Mrs. Kolitas finished up.

She greeted him cheerfully, hurrying around the room, making the bed, rinsing out his few breakfast dishes, and sweeping the sand off the floor. Luke did not bother to engage Mrs. Kolitas in any conversation; her English consisted of only a few words. He smiled, offering a greeting in Greek, and sat down at his desk to work. Even as he forced himself to write, successfully ignoring Mrs. Kolitas's movements around the room, he could not shake the weird presentiment of doom still hanging on from that awful nightmare.

When the cleaning woman left, Luke pushed

his papers aside. He was too on edge to work. The coffee was only lukewarm now, but he poured himself a second cup.

He heard a knock on his door and opened it to find a pale, sober-looking Dodger Roy standing on the front step. He almost dropped the cup of coffee out of his hand.

First that nightmare, and now Cat's father. Luke was visibly shaken.

Dodger, seeing the effect his presence had on Luke, quickly assured him nothing was wrong—yet.

"Yet?"

"I had a visit this morning from Liz Fuller. She's the star—"

"I know. What did she say?"

"Well, you see, there's this gag we have planned for this afternoon. A wild chase around Skiros— you know the island?"

"I haven't been there. It's a good three or four hours from this island if you're lucky enough to get a ferry."

"We chose it because it's got the right setup and it's not too populated. There's no problem getting the roads cleared to do the stunt."

"Another car crash into brick walls?" Luke could not disguise the sarcastic bite to his voice.

Dodger sighed. "Car crashes are 'in' this year. Everyone's trying to outdo everyone else in these suspense yarns with bigger, better, and more daring chase scenes. They want the audience falling off the edge of their seats, and my crew is the group that's supposed to make that happen. This

231

time around we eliminate brick walls; you never repeat the same gag for two pictures in a row. If I did that, I would be out of a job."

"What exactly are you worried about?" Luke asked pointedly.

"Well, I have to admit it's only a gut feeling. But I just can't seem to shake it off."

Luke was all too familiar with that feeling today.

"Liz told me she was pretty sure Cat was secretly planning a dangerous trick in today's stunt. I confronted Cat before coming over here, and she swears she changed her mind after sleeping on it. I don't believe her."

"I'd trust your instinct," Luke said. "Just what is she planning?"

"Yesterday, while we were running through the stunt, Cat tells me she wants to add this crazy piece of daredevil business to her drive. I vetoed it cold. The last time a guy did something similar, he broke half the bones in his body. And that was only because he was lucky and the car wasn't rigged with explosives. If Cat tried that stunt and goofed, it would not be broken bones we'd be talking about."

"But if you vetoed it, how can she go ahead with it?"

"Luke, you must know Cat pretty well by now." He grinned. "She's always been stubborn and dead set on getting her own way. Usually, I can manage the upper hand with her. But this time . . . She's been in one hell of a bad mood these past few days. I don't think she's thinking straight, that's for sure. That rebellious spirit in her is something else right now. I don't mean to pry, but did you two have a fight or something?"

"We didn't have a fight. We had a calm, rational, intelligent discussion about the impossibility of our relationship. We both agreed it made sense to end it now before we got in any deeper." Luke's voice was tight, his chin contracting as he spoke.

"I see." Dodger rubbed his jaw, his eyes on Luke's. "You both figured it was for the best?"

"Right." Luke's response lacked conviction. How could feeling this miserable be best?

"I'm pretty sure she's in love with you. But I guess you know that. I was hoping, with her feeling the way she does about you, maybe you could talk some sense into her before she went and did something crazy. But I guess you've done all your talking already."

"You sure know how to dig in there, Dodger." Luke smirked. "Can't you stop her? Take her off the stunt if you believe she's going to pull something."

"Without proof? I can't do that. And I can't stop her following through on her plan. When a stunter steps into that car and the camera starts to roll, I lose all control. Sure, I told Cat I'd have her blackballed if she pulled that extra fancy maneuver. She looked me straight in the eye, with this innocent smile on that pretty little face of hers, and told me flat out that she wouldn't go against my wishes. Well, now, when Cat gives you one of those sweet smiles, you know something is cooking in that head of hers. I don't think she has any intention of following my orders. Now, like I said, I could be wrong . . ."

"But neither of us think you are."

Dodger nodded. "That's about it. I came all this distance because I believe if she'd listen to anyone, she'd listen to you."

"You're wrong, Dodger. She's known all along how I feel about those stunts. And to be perfectly honest with you, I can't really face watching her go through another one. Each time I feel certain she's about to kill herself. But like she told me— she never even gets a scratch."

"Well, this time, my friend, your fears are justified. I told you Cat was the best female stunter in the business. She's been the best because she's put herself one hundred percent into what she is doing. And she never got into something over her head before. She's got two strikes against her on this one. I think her heart is here with you . . . and her head is sinking in deep water."

Luke knew he would not be able to stop her. He also knew he had to go with Dodger and try, anyway.

CHAPTER FOURTEEN

"What time did you say that stunt was called for?" Luke asked, his eye on his watch as they waited for the ferry.

"Three o'clock, bar no hang-ups. The later, the better. These ferries are never on schedule." Dodger shook his head, trying to keep calm. In his business, a cool head was something you either learned early on, or you found some other line of work. Today, he never felt more like he should be out looking for a different way to earn a living.

Luke had to keep a cool head in his business, too. But he was having as much difficulty staying calm as Dodger. He still doubted that he could stop Cat, even if the ferries got them there on time. And that event in itself was not too likely. They needed to take one ferry to Alonnisos and then hook up with a second one to Skiros. On those rare days both ferries ran on schedule it was a three-hour trip.

It was eleven o'clock. They had that one-hour leeway but that was it. And if this ferry was late and the one from Alonnisos on time, they would be stranded. That was the only ferry that day out to Skiros.

The ferry was due in at eleven-fifteen. No one waiting on the small dock with the exception of Luke and Dodger seemed particularly perturbed that it hadn't arrived. Worse than that, Luke couldn't make it out on the horizon.

He walked over to a robust, darkly tanned man dressed in large trousers and a thin cotton work shirt, and who was selling ferry tickets.

"Any idea when that ferry will get here?" he asked him.

The man gave him a friendly nod. "It will come. It usually does."

Terrific. Luke groaned. But when? Luke shrugged and walked off, doubting he would have learned anything more, anyway. By eleven-thirty Luke and Dodger were not bothering to hide their edginess.

"We're getting down to the wire, Luke. What do you think?"

More people had gathered for the ferry. They must have known they had every chance of making it despite arriving late. The boat was still nowhere in sight.

"I think we'd better see if we can get to Alonnisos some other way. Maybe somebody here will take

236

us across in a trawler," Luke suggested, scanning the area for a likely possibility.

"I'd settle for a rowboat. Only I don't think we'd make it in time. The thing to do is find us a fast little motor launch." Dodger pointed to one tied up at dock.

"How do we find out who owns it?"

"That's the problem. My Greek is limited to a few menu items. How about you?"

Luke shrugged. "Maybe the guy who sells the tickets can help."

When he walked back over to the ticket seller, the man was deep into a conversation with a small, frail-looking elderly woman who, despite the near one-hundred-degree temperature, wore a long-sleeved black dress and matching black kerchief neatly knotted under her chin. She was carrying a large wicker basket that Luke guessed must be quite heavy, yet the woman seemed to have no difficulty managing it.

The ticket seller looked up at Luke and smiled. "My mother," the man explained, his eyebrows raised.

Luke smiled. In some ways, Greece was no different from other places. Mothers were mothers the world wide.

"You are anxious to get to Alonnisos, yes?"

"Very anxious."

He turned to his mother and said something in rapid Greek that made her smile.

"Even on vacations Americans are in a hurry." He had a good laugh over his own observation, leisurely wiping the sweat off his brow with the palm of his hand.

"Sometimes when it is hot like this, the engine on that broken-down ferry goes crazy. It doesn't feel like making such an effort—back and forth, then back and forth again. You want to go to Athens? That ferry is much bigger, newer. You will have a good time in Athens."

"Look, I need to get to Alonnisos. It is very important. I—I'm a doctor and there is—"

"A doctor! Why didn't you say that?" He turned again to his mother to explain. This time she nodded slowly, her eyes moving to Luke.

"Dimitris," he called over to another man on the dock, then turned to Luke. "Go with him, Doctor. He will get you to your patient. That ferry . . . I tell you, one of these days they'll have to get another."

Luke motioned to Dodger, the two of them rushing over to Dimitris, who had donned his captain's hat.

Dimitris spoke no English. He led the two men to his small fishing trawler and spent what felt like an eternity readying the boat for the trip. However, Luke and Dodger were so relieved to be aboard anything that had a chance of making it across to Alonnisos they were not going to let their frustration get the better of them.

The water was choppy, the boat riding the waves with a surprisingly pristine grace. Despite its appearance, it turned out to be a worthy little seagoing vessel.

Luke kept shifting his gaze from his watch to the broad expanse of sea stretched out in front of him. Alonnisos was visible in the distance—a tiny, shimmering diamond in the early-afternoon sun.

Dodger was glad of his decision to get Luke and bring him to Skiros. Joanie had been the one to bring it up first. When Liz Fuller had left the bungalow this morning, Dodger was in a rip-roaring fit. Joanie calmed him down and forced him to think constructively about how to stop Cat from carrying out this stunt. Dodger wanted to go after the mechanics, tell them if they touched Cat's car beyond his specs, he would have them all fired. Joanie pointed out that Cat would try the stunt, anyway, if she got angry enough. And she might, if Dodger got into a strong battle of wills with his daughter.

Joanie did manage to calm him down, which was not an easy feat. Joanie was the best thing that had ever happened to him in his life. It sometimes made him literally ill at the thought that he had been almost pigheaded enough to lose her. Here he'd been worrying about the fact that he was so much older than her, only to discover in some ways she was more mature and wiser than him.

He agreed that Joanie's idea to get Luke to talk reason into Cat was a good bet. But he was hesitant about going after him. It was clear Luke and Cat had had some kind of a fight. He never got in the middle of other people's battles, especially not his daughter's. Maybe the doc was out for a little fling, nothing more. Then again, maybe that was all Cat had wanted. But his own impression from that evening they'd all had dinner together was that both Luke and his daughter were running away from some far more serious feelings. Dodger understood that fear from his own experience.

Luke drew a quiet breath of relief when they were in clear sight of the island. Dimitris pointed to a small dock where he could easily let them off and swing his trawler back around.

It was eleven-fifty. The ferry dock was only a few minutes from where they were being let out. They both shook hands with the captain, who smiled profusely and refused the money Dodger tried to offer him.

They made a run for it. Luke could feel his pulse pounding in his ears. He'd let himself go to hell these past few weeks. He was going to have to get back into shape.

Dodger was doing a bit of huffing and puffing, too. Being a stunt coordinator did not give you the same physical workout stunting did.

They were only a hundred yards from the ferry dock when they saw the boat.

"Come on, Luke. We've got to put on some speed." Dodger shouted off to his side as he heard the horn blast.

Damn it, Luke thought, running faster, the one time you want the ferry to be delayed a couple of minutes, and it decides today's the day it's going to surprise everyone and leave a couple of minutes early.

The boat's engines grew louder. Slowly, it pulled

out of shore. The two men were maybe fifteen yards from the ferry. Luke started to slow up. What was the point? They'd missed it by seconds.

Dodger grabbed hold of Luke's wrist. "You ever done a stunt before, Doc?"

"Huh?" Luke was being jettisoned forward by Dodger's powerful tug.

"There's nothing to it, Doc. We're going to take a real easy running broad jump. Hold on."

"Dodger, you're crazy! We'll never make it. *I'll* never make it." But he kept running.

When Luke's feet left the wooden dock he had a fleeting image of a bird soaring into space. He prayed his wings would hold out as he sailed over the water toward the boat. It had to have been a stretch of over twelve feet. As Luke touched the solid ground of the ferry's deck, he felt both the thrill of success and the terror of having almost landed on those churning blades cutting through the water.

Dodger looked over at Luke and grinned. "You've got an innate talent for stunting, Doc. But something tells me it's not a skill you want to develop."

Cat had won. Everything was going according to her plan. She walked down to the garage to check on her car one last time.

Bill was giving the Porsche a final once-over, and when he saw Cat approach, he nodded that everything was as ordered. He didn't smile as he usually did. A sullen, worried expression replaced his normally sunny disposition. Cat was getting

241

used to that look. She was seeing it on everyone's face since she'd decided to go ahead on this stunt.

This morning Peter had come down to her cottage to talk with her about the stunt again. She knew he was having misgivings before he said a word.

"Cat, I've connived for some risky stunts on my pictures. You know my reputation and you know a few of the fellows that have broken an arm or leg pulling some gag off. I accept the fact that it's a dangerous business, and I realize there's always a risk when a stunter goes out to do any gag. But I've never had somebody seriously injure themselves on any picture I've ever directed. Certainly no one has died. Cat, don't do this if you have even a fraction of a doubt. It isn't worth it. I'm not bucking for an award won over spilled blood."

"Peter, I don't have any doubts at all. And I'm not going to spill any of my blood. I promise. The way I've got that car rigged, it can't roll over. We're going to take a pretty two-wheeled slide that's going to look a hell of a lot harder to manage than it really is. Believe me, Peter. I do know what I'm doing."

"I hope so, Cat. I sure hope so."

Cat patted him on the back and led him to the door. After he left, she walked down to a nearby beach. Staying at the compound meant bumping into other upset people like Liz, Joanie, and Dodger. She knew she wasn't pulling the wool over her father's eyes, just as she knew there was no way to stop her. Cat was banking on the fact that once she pulled off this stunt, he would come around. That's what had happened in San Francisco when he had finally consented to letting her do Ben's tricky crash gag. It was all going to work out—at least as far as her career was concerned.

Another notch on her belt. Another amazing accomplishment. She was a woman in a man's world pulling her equal weight. And after this stunt today, there would not be a single coordinator or director who would doubt her ability to stand in for any stunt required. That was what she wanted, wasn't it? It had been her dream since childhood—what she had fantasized about when she watched her father perform his daredevil feats.

So where was the excitement, the heady anticipation? All she had accomplished so far was to alienate everyone she loved.

She sat down on the sand, along the water's edge, letting the rivulets of water tickle her bare feet. She missed Luke with a pain that wouldn't let up. She missed the feel of his embrace, the sound of his laughter, his whispered words of pleasure as she surprised and delighted him. She missed his gentle, tender warmth. She missed his love.

They had given that love freely, but once it had been discussed openly, they had both gotten scared. She and Luke were independent, self-contained people, sure of themselves, sure of where they were heading. The only thing they weren't in the least bit sure of was how loving each other, making a commitment to nurture that love, would affect their lives. And they were both scared to find out.

Luke would bury himself in his work and Cat would bury herself in hers. Really, it was no different than before they'd ever met. But before then, neither of them had ever experienced what it felt like to be jealous. They had never been in love before. Their goals were uncomplicated, unencumbered.

She had been so confident of what she wanted. She had always told herself there was plenty of time to fall in love, to settle down. But then she discovered that love had no time schedule.

At the garage, watching Bill make some final adjustments to her car, she forced her mind back to the task at hand.

"It's looking good, Bill," she said, forcing a cheery note in her voice, afraid it might betray the faint doubt that clung to her. Why was she really doing this? What did she want to prove? Could pushing herself into bigger and riskier stunts help her forget the gnawing pain in her gut, the emptiness that engulfed her?

"I've checked it over a half-dozen times, Cat. Every single sharp object's been torn out of the car. I've triple-reinforced all the padding. We'll make sure there's only enough gas in the tank to run the stunt. It's those damned explosives that are giving me nightmares. I even welded in an extra roll bar. If the car does go over, at least she'll only rock like a cradle, possibly—just possibly—

preventing the explosives from going off on impact. But I can't give you good odds, Cat."

"Bill, you've thought of everything. I'm not going to need those odds, because I'm not rolling this baby over." She patted the hood of the car.

"Well, I wouldn't want to be in your shoes—or should I say, your asbestos suit. God, I sure hope there aren't any early fireworks from this beauty." He glanced from Cat to the sleek, silver sportscar that would, after Cat leaped to safety, collide with the other two cars, and all three would burst into flames.

"Has Dodger been by?" she asked, spotting the flicker of consternation on Bill's face.

"He came down for a minute, but he didn't double-check the car. He said he had some business to attend to on one of the other islands this morning and would be back for the stunt at three."

"What kind of business?"

Bill shrugged, but Cat had a pretty good idea Dodger had headed for Skiathos to have a heart to heart with Dr. Luke Eliot about his crazy daughter. What was he hoping to gain?

Cat strode out of the garage and went hunting for Peter Whitney. She had one more change she wanted to make.

The ferry to Skiros took two hours on good days. This was not one of them. The boat had been adrift in the middle of the sea for the last twenty minutes as the engineer tried to get it going again. Luke and Dodger had no idea what was wrong, but they did know that if it wasn't fixed soon, their whole madcap race against time would be a complete bust.

"Don't ask me the time again, Dodger. It's five minutes later than the last time you asked." Luke got up from the bench and walked over to the railing. He turned back to face Dodger.

"Why the hell does Cat want to do this?" Then, before Dodger could respond, he went on, "It's my profession to understand what makes people tick, but for the life of me, since I met Cat, I haven't been able to figure out what makes either one of us tick." He sat back down next to Dodger, shaking his head, rubbing his jaw. "I didn't even shave this morning," he said abruptly. "I always used to shave first thing in the morning. A habit of mine since I went off to college." That morning at the Drake Hotel flashed in his mind. He had to smile, remembering how he had stopped to grab a shave in the men's room before showing up at that medical conference. "Now I forget to shave; I'm unable to concentrate on my work for more than a few minutes at a stretch without Cat popping up in my mind; I'm watching her do these crazy stunts; and I'm even doing some of my own. No one I know would believe I'm the same person anymore. I can't believe it myself."

"Listen," Dodger said, looking across at Luke, "I've found out myself that love does strange things to people. Shakes you right up. Makes you have to rethink a million thoughts you figured were nice and clear in your mind. Turns you topsy-turvy."

"Well put." Luke grinned.

"You know what I would do if I were in your shoes, Doc? I'd grab hold of that little girl, shake some sense into that stubborn head of hers, and then I'd perform one more stunt. I'd get a good grip on her, throw her over my shoulder, and run like the dickens until she stopped kicking and bucking."

"You really think that would work?" The fact that he would seriously consider doing just that confirmed in his own mind that he must be going nuts.

Dodger sighed. "Nothing else has. I'd sure as hell help clear the way for you." He smiled.

Luke never got the opportunity to find out if carrying Cat off would have done any good.

The boat, after what felt like endless hours at sea, finally pulled into the dock at Skiros at two-thirty. They still had half an hour, and they were less than ten minutes from the starting point of the chase scene. They ran, anyway. It was not going to be easy to get hold of Cat and talk her out of her extra fancy maneuvering.

The roads had been cordoned off for the shoot, a few locals guarding the barriers. Fortunately, one of them recognized Dodger from the day before when he had run through the stunt with Cat and the two stunt men.

Even before they rounded the bend, Luke and Dodger heard the revving up of engines.

"What the hell . . . ?" Dodger broke into a faster run, Luke trailing just behind.

Joanie spotted them and came running over. "Oh, Dodger, you're too late. Cat must have gotten suspicious that you'd try to do something to stop her, and she got Whitney to move up the stunt half an hour."

"When I get my hands on that girl . . ." *If* he got his hands on her, he thought, a sick feeling attacking his stomach.

Luke was speechless. All he could do was shake his head back and forth. Dodger grabbed his arm and led him over to a Jeep. "We'd better get down to where she's going to pull off that stunt!" he shouted.

The ride took only five minutes, both men silent as they drove. The odds had been against them all along. Now they could only hope the odds were with Cat. When Luke glanced over at Dodger, he saw etched lines of fear on the older man's face. He didn't know that those same lines were etched on his.

Five minutes before Luke and Dodger arrived on the scene, Cat swept her hair off her neck, pinning it up with a barrette, and took the helmet Bill handed her. She slipped it on her head, adjusting the goggles over her eyes. Concentrating on breathing evenly, she got her pulse rate under control.

Bill gave the car one last pat, then bent down and said to Cat, "You can always change your mind before you get to that spot, Cat. It would still be a great chase and you'd make a lot of people mighty happy."

Cat nodded, but he knew she had no intention of pulling out. Cat would go through with whatever she set her mind on. Still, he'd felt the need to say his piece.

The two stunt men involved in the chase got into their respective cars. They had been told to hold back an extra two minutes to give Cat clearance to do her thing. Either of the stunters would have gone in her place, yet neither of them could say they envied her. Don Reevers had been one of the stunt men in *Deathwatch*, and had been there the day George Corey tried this stunt. But Corey had misjudged that shoulder and the car had spun wildly out of control. He had managed to get out before the car hit the guardrail, but instead of landing on the well-packed earth, he careened across the pavement and broke four or five ribs in the process. No, he sure didn't envy Cat Roy.

She felt a momentary flash of nervousness, a tiny flicker of doubt, but then she shook her mind free of everything but getting her car to do exactly what she wanted.

The first stretch of the road required a few swerves, some near-collisions with the other two cars chasing her. For ten seconds she had to maneuver out of the sandwich as the stunters came up on either side of her.

Cat pressed her foot down on the accelerator and shot out of the wedge. Don spun his car within inches of a stationary cart while the other driver edged close to the side of the cliff road. Cat kept her speed up as she shot down the long straightaway. The whole while Peter rode in the lead car with the cameraman, who was getting every move down on film. Peter watched and prayed. They were nearing the sweeping corner.

Cat took the corner and got ready for that shoulder bank in the road. She was cool and calm as she slowed down slightly and edged the car onto the shoulder. It felt good. She was going to carry it off with style. A smile flashed on her face.

In an instant the smile vanished. She had checked everything in her control. The road was perfect, having been gone over with a fine-tooth comb. The car was performing better than she could have hoped. She was feeling terrific coming onto the shoulder, certain the car would tip sideways at just the right angle, so that she could right it back on all fours, send it into its spin, and get out.

The one thing that was not in her control, or anybody's, was the weather. As she started to tip, she realized that a plain old tail wind blowing straight down toward the car was going to throw her calculations off by a fraction. And it was only a fraction that was going to keep the car from its sideways trip to a calamitous rollover position. Cat put one gloved hand on the door handle. She might have to make an earlier escape than planned.

Dodger's Jeep stood among three tow trucks and a makeshift ambulance. A local doctor from the town was also standing nearby. The sight did not fill Luke with confidence.

Dodger had briefly explained what Cat was going to do. The very thought of pulling off that kind of maneuver seemed impossible to Luke. Dodger tried to sound reassuring, but he was not convincing.

Don't let anything happen to her, he prayed silently, his hands clenched at his side, his eyes glued to the spot where she was supposed to tip the car sideways and right it again. She's a pro, he kept reminding himself. She can do it. She has to do it.

She rounded the curve.

"That a girl. Nice and easy. Slow it down," Dodger whispered. "Edge it up. Good . . ."

The last word died in his throat.

They all watched the car begin to tip. Dodger already understood the problem, helpless to do anything about it. Luke had no idea why things had gone wrong, but he stood by, equally helpless, as the car continued in hideous slow motion to go from its side completely over on to the roof and then slide inexorably toward the guardrail.

CHAPTER FIFTEEN

Cat's lucky charm, in the form of Luke Eliot, must have been working for her. Or else it was a pure miracle, though temporary at best. The car, skidding on its roof, slid to a stop against the guardrail. The movement of the vehicle had been slow enough not to trigger off the explosion, but it could go at any moment.

The big problem was that Cat's side of the car was wedged against the rail, preventing her exit. The passenger's side had jammed shut in the initial rollover.

Any movement of the car to get her out could set off the explosive. Cat was pinned in her seat. She was unharmed, but she could not reach the charger to disconnect it.

"Clear the area. Don't get anywhere near that car. It could go any second!" Cole Jenkins, the head of special effects, shouted the warning into the crowd.

Dodger was already racing to the scene, Luke a couple of feet behind him. Jenkins caught hold of Luke's arm.

"Hold it, buddy. You've got to keep back."

"I'm a doctor. Let go of me." Luke wrenched himself free.

There was a small group over at the car—Peter Whitney, the other two stunt drivers, and two of the mechanics. Dodger, after checking to make sure Cat was all right, was conferring with the other men about the best way to get into the car, while jarring it as little as possible in the process.

Luke bent down at the passenger window. It was closed, so he had to shout.

"Are you hurt, Cat?"

She gave him a thumbs-up sign that in her upside-down position was actually thumbs-down. "I'm fine. Just getting a wee bit dizzy, and it's a little stuffy in here," she said, managing a smile.

Luke could see the strain in her features; her eyes were wide with fear, despite her brave attempt to remain calm.

"We're going to get you out, Cat."

"I know. I'm okay, really. Leave this to the pros, Luke. Please, don't stay so close."

"I'm not budging until you're out."

Dodger came over. "Okay, baby, here's what we're gonna do. Your side got jammed into the railing, and we don't want to risk pulling on the car. So we'll get that trunk open and get you out that way. Just hold on. Don has to work on it for a minute. It got a little crushed when you rolled."

"Take it slow, Dodger." She forced a grin.

"You bet, little girl."

Luke followed Dodger around to the back of the car.

"There really is nothing you can do, Luke. Why don't you go wait over at the side of the road?"

"What are the chances of getting her out without setting off the explosion?"

Dodger wiped his brow, staring off in the distance for a moment as though looking for an answer. He brought his gaze back to Luke. "I wish to God I knew."

Don was working on the trunk lock. His movements were painstakingly slow. Luke wished he could go faster, but he knew time was not the only element working against them. Any force could set off that charge.

Everyone on the set had heard by now, and they were all gathered along the side of the road, two of the crew making sure they stayed far enough back from the accident. Liz and Joanie stood together, their eyes glued to the car.

They all watched, a silent vigil, as the men worked on the car.

"How are you doing, Don?"

The mechanic looked up at the sound of Dodger's voice.

"I don't know if we can get her open without exerting too much pressure."

254

"Keep working on it, real easy. I have another idea."

Dodger swung a leg over the guardrail and edged over to Cat's side of the car. With just sheer cliff below him, he clung to the rail as he bent low.

"Any chance you can roll down your window?" If she could get the window open, he could rig some rope and pull her out that way.

Cat shook her head, then quickly looked across to the other window. When she saw that Luke wasn't there, she turned back to Dodger. "My arm is pinned against the door, Dodger. I can't move it. Even if you get that trunk open, I don't know how you're going to get me free." She tried desperately to keep the note of panic out of her voice. She wasn't altogether successful. Neither was Dodger at keeping the look of fear from his face.

"We're going to get you out. Just hold on a little longer."

He knew what he had to do. The risk was high, but there was no other alternative. They couldn't move the car, but they might be able to work on that rail.

Dodger hurriedly gave out orders. Three more men joined the group and flew into action. Rope was carefully set around the car and attached to Dodger's Jeep to keep it from moving right over the cliff when the guardrail was removed. Then more rope was knotted to the railings to the left and right of the one that had to be freed. The ropes were rigged into a contraption that held two men. At either end of the car the men set to work using hacksaws to cut the railing. Blowtorches would be faster but much too dangerous.

The car shifted slightly. Luke was again at the passenger window. He felt helpless. All he could do was offer Cat moral support and hope she didn't pass out from her inverted position or pure fear.

Cat saw him and somehow felt more hopeful. "Remember that day I said if I ever was in real danger I'd want you around? Guess my wish came true," she said with a sardonic smile.

Luke had to grin. He wouldn't have to worry about her spirits. Not that he didn't know that she was scared, but she was probably holding up better than anyone. Certainly better than he.

One side of the railing was finally freed. Now came the tricky part. The door handle had wedged into the metal railing on collision. Before the men could fully saw through the other end, they had to pry the railing back as carefully as possible to prevent jarring the car too much when the other end was completely freed.

Dodger waited, his eyes never leaving that galvanized metal railing, while the two men worked together to detach the handle from the thick metal rod without exerting too much force. The car again shifted, but finally the men managed to free the rail and set to work quickly finishing up the sawing. When their job was safely accomplished, they were pulled back over to the road.

The Jeep kept the car from sliding over the precipice, but the tough part was far from over. Dodger tied the rope to his waist. Now he had to get Cat's door open. He prayed the crash had not made the task too difficult.

"Almost there, little girl. Almost there." He reached for the mangled door handle and tried it. No give.

Cat, her eyes wide, stared at her father's face. "Maybe I can help, Dodger." With her free hand, she pressed her palm against the inside of the door. "Try again. I'll push as you tug."

"Not too hard now," he reminded her.

She nodded. "Say when."

Luke saw one of the crew start to put the extra rope around his waist to go help Dodger.

"I'll do it," Luke said, stopping the man in mid-motion.

"I don't think . . ."

Dodger looked over. "It's okay, Don. He's done a couple of stunts with me before." He managed a quick grin to Luke, watching him carefully edge over to his side. He felt better having Luke's help because they both would do anything they could to help Cat.

When Cat saw Luke at her window, her eyes grew wider with fear. But there was also love mirrored in her gaze. Luke smiled at her, giving her a thumbs-up sign.

"We're all going to work together now, nice and easy. Don't force the door. Let's just see if we can get it open without too much trouble," Dodger said loudly, making sure Cat heard him clearly.

Luke dug his feet into the cliff to give himself more stability. He placed his two hands on the door handle while Dodger wedged his fingers into the rim of the door window. Cat kept her palm pressed flat against the inside of the door.

Whether it was a miracle or just plain luck, the door gave way on the count of three. Luke had the toughest job then. He had to immediately let go of the handle as soon as the door began to move so as not to jerk the car and blow them all to smithereens. He pushed off with his feet and grabbed on to the guardrail to his left. Meanwhile, Dodger quickly undid Cat's seat belt and caught her by the waist, carefully helping her out of the car and into his arms. As soon as she was securely in his grasp, Dodger gave the okay and they were pulled to safety.

Luke swung himself over the guardrail and rushed over to Cat. Only then did he realize she had injured her arm in the crash. He saw blood all over her elbow and forearm. There wasn't time to do anything but run for cover with the others. As soon as they were all free of the car, the ropes attaching it to the Jeep were removed. The car fell over the precipice and crashed in an explosive burst of flames at the bottom of the cliff.

Cat was being bandaged up by the local physician. Fortunately, the wound was not deep, and the gash did not even require stitches.

"Nice little gag you performed out there." She grinned as Luke sat beside her.

The full impact of what they had all just been through was first coming to the surface for Luke. When he reached out to brush a wayward strand

258

of hair from Cat's face, his hand was trembling badly.

"I don't want to reshoot it—ever," he said in a low, husky voice. "And don't ever try telling me this crazy business isn't dangerous."

"I guess I shouldn't have added that extra little spark. I was so sure I had everything figured to the letter. Actually, it wasn't my fault. The wind went against me at the last minute. Next time I'll—"

"Next time?" His voice held disbelief.

"You won't have to reshoot, darling, but I will. Don't look so panicked. I'm going to follow orders next time and do the stunt the way Dodger asked me to do it in the first place. There's no danger . . ."

Luke stared at her, shock and anger in his eyes. "When do you stop? After the bomb goes off and there's nothing left of you to carry out the next insane stunt? How many times do you have to look death in the eye before you realize you've had enough?"

"Luke, listen—"

"No. *You* listen. I will never put myself through this again. Do you understand, Cat? I love you. Today has made me realize that more than ever. Your life is precious to me. But it has to be precious to you, too. You have to value it enough to give up stunting. We'd have a real chance then, Cat. Sure, there are other issues, but I know we could surmount any obstacle if you remove this one."

"Luke, I can't just walk out on all of this. I—I know how scared you were."

"What about you? Don't pretend you weren't terrified. I saw the look in your eyes. Cat, you are a courageous, strong, determined woman. I love you for that. I'm proud of the brave way you coped with that near disaster. There's no need to keep proving it."

"You keep accusing me of trying to prove something. I'm not."

"Then let somebody else do that stunt. And all the rest of them. Walk out now. Or else I will. I mean it, Cat."

"I—I can't quit just like that."

"Yes, you can. If that's what you want."

She looked up at him as he stood. Her eyes filled with tears as they met his. "I can't run away."

He nodded slowly, his gaze reflecting pain and sorrow. "Good-bye, Cat."

Only then did he see Dodger standing nearby. He gave him a sad smile and walked away.

Cat looked over at her father. The tears fell freely.

"Go after him, little girl. He's worth it." Dodger came up to Cat as he spoke.

"It won't work, Dodger. Not this way. What kind of a life would we have together if we both knew he had blackmailed me into giving up my career?"

He sat down next to her, holding her hand as

she cried softly for a few minutes. Joanie had started to come over, but seeing what was happening, she met Dodger's eyes in understanding and turned away.

When Cat got her tears under control, Dodger said softly, "You look like you could use a drink. Come to think of it, so could I." He gave her a broad grin. "That little stunt gave me quite a thirst."

He reached for her hand, put his arm around her, and guided her over to his Jeep.

When the others saw Cat and Dodger, they understood that this was a time for father and daughter to be alone. Dodger winked at Joanie, who then joined Peter and Liz in the director's car.

When Dodger drove off, Cat took one last look at the gaping hole in the guardrail. It had been a stomach-wrenching episode for all of them, Cat admitted. Luke had been right. She had been terrified while pinned upside down in that death trap. Hundreds of thoughts ran through her mind as she was held poised at the edge of that precipice, never sure whether she was going to get out of this thing alive. Some of her thoughts had been the same as Luke's. This was a crazy way to earn a living. It was more dangerous than she had ever accepted before. Never before had she come this close to death.

She thought, too, about Dodger warning her in the past not to start feeling invincible. That was exactly what had happened to her, despite her promise that it never would. Well, after today's experience she would never believe she was invincible again.

Other thoughts came into sharp focus as she was pinned to that seat. Thoughts of Luke. Thoughts about how very much she loved him. She didn't want the fantasy to end. It had become too vital, too real. And not just for her, she realized now. Luke had risked his life for her. He could have stood on the sidelines, but he didn't.

Dodger parked in front of a small roadside taverna. He led her to a patio table that was shaded by a large umbrella. When the waiter came over, he ordered ouzo and water for them both.

"Peter isn't going to be too happy about having to use a second car." Cat stared down at the table as she spoke. "I'm sorry, Dodger. It was so dumb. I don't know what got into me. When you told me I couldn't do the stunt my way . . . I don't know, something snapped inside of me. Luke is probably right. I seem hell-bent to prove I can do any stunt that I dream up."

"You've got to stop dreaming so much, little girl. Maybe you've got to start thinking some more about what you're really after."

Cat's blue eyes were tinged with confusion and sadness. "I don't know anymore. I was scared today, Dodger. I keep thinking, though, that if I give in to that fear it will control me. When something like this happens, you either get right back up on that horse—or back in the car in this case—or you'll never ride again. Isn't that true, Dodger?"

He had to admit it was true. And he couldn't honestly advise Cat to quit in this way, spending her life with the knowledge that she had fled in terror.

"Do you remember your mother very much, Cat?"

She looked over at Dodger in surprise. "Mom? Not very well. Hardly at all, really. I do remember how sad my fourth birthday was without her."

"Luke's feelings about you being in the business remind me a lot of her's. She hated this business—right from the start."

"But she married you, Dodger. She had to know what she was getting into."

He patted his daughter's hand. "I was quite persuasive in those days. I met your mother while I was stunting for a B picture in Chicago. Can't even remember which one. It doesn't matter. I was restless one evening and went out with a couple of friends to a small club in town. I was sitting, drinking my beer, and minding my business when I heard a lady arguing with this fellow. Seems the man had too much to drink and was getting way out of line with his date. To make a long story short, I knocked the guy out and took your mother home that night. Saw her every night after that for the three weeks I was in town."

"I never did know how the two of you met. You never used to want to speak about her before."

Dodger looked steadily at Cat. "It was wrong of me, Cat. I should have told you a lot of things. First I was too bitter, then too guilty. When your mom walked out on me and took you with her back to Chicago, I was fit to be tied. Just like you just said . . . she married me knowing what I did for a living."

His voice was soft as he went on. "It was really a crazy business in those days. All the technical sophistication we use today barely existed then. A lot of people didn't know what the hell they were doing. Half the time, I probably didn't . . . although I wouldn't have admitted anything of the sort back then. I sure never admitted it to your mother, any more than I told her about all the guys being shipped off to hospitals or morgues. But she knew, anyway. She saw the whole picture early on, and she didn't like what she saw one bit."

"She asked you to quit?"

"A hundred times. She even walked out on me before you were born. The thing of it was, we were crazy about each other. She came back a week later. But nothing was any different. Then you came along, and she was more adamant than ever. It came down to a final ultimatum."

"This is beginning to sound familiar," Cat said with a wry smile.

"Yep. And I handled it just the way you did. I wasn't going to be blackmailed, either."

"Are you telling me now you were wrong?" she asked, doubting she could be convinced.

"We were both wrong . . . and we were both right. What it boiled down to was that we both suffered. It just about broke my heart when she walked out that last time, you in tow. I was losing both of you. Then, on top of all the pain, your mom got sick. . . ." Dodger swallowed hard, shaking his head. "I sure did want you back, little girl . . . but not that way. Thank God she didn't suffer much. The cancer took over her body so fast, no one had time to prepare for her leaving us. Her father told me she passed away quietly in her sleep less than a week after they found out what was wrong with her."

Cat squeezed Dodger's hand. She had only the faintest memory of her mother, mostly honed from the few photographs she had of her. Cat vaguely remembered the funeral, everyone crying, her father holding her in his arms. She didn't know until long afterward how Dodger had fought her grandparents for custody of her. Dodger might not have won if it wasn't for her grandpa's bad heart condition. "Would you have done things differently, if you had a chance to do them over?" she asked quietly.

"I thought about that question myself, many times. I don't know if it would have really changed anything, but yes . . . I would have done things differently."

"You would have quit?"

"Cat, when I was your age, I saw everything in such black-and-white terms. Like I think you see things now. Maybe it's only with age that you come to realize that life has a lot of gray in it. Those few years with your mom I fought for things to be one way . . . my way. What that did, I realize now, was back her into a corner. I pushed with all my strength in one direction, and she pushed with all her power in the opposite direction. We ended up in a stalemate. And that's where we were both wrong."

Dodger smiled. "There's a word I added to my vocabulary too late to work things out with your mother. The word is compromise, Cat. I intend to put that word to use every chance I get with Joanie."

"Even if I was able to compromise, Dodger, I'm not sure Luke could. I don't think he believes in compromise in this situation. As he sees it, all stunts are death-defying feats. He's as adamant about this being a black-and-white issue as Mom was with you. You heard him yourself."

"I heard a man who just went through a mighty rough experience. He saw your car roll over. He almost witnessed the woman he loves get blown to smithereens. At this moment he probably can't see much beyond that."

"I guess you're right. But I'm not very confident he'll ever be able to see the color 'gray' on this one."

"Give him a chance to settle down a bit and go find out."

Cat smiled hesitantly. "I think I'm more frightened to do that than to get back in another Porsche and replay the crash scene."

"Yeah . . . but accomplishing the first may be worth a lot more to you than smashing up some car in a perfectly executed stunt."

"You've got a point there, Dodger. But I can't seem to stop calculating the odds. What would I say to him? I don't want to lose him. I love him. I'll never find anyone like him ever again."

She sighed, staring down at her untouched glass of ouzo. "Sometimes I wish he'd never seen me perched on the ledge that day. I feel like I'm on a giant roller coaster—up one minute, and the next, I'm hurtling downward, barely holding on. I'm sure it feels the same way to Luke."

"Joanie and I took one of those rough rides, too," Dodger said.

"But somehow you were able to get off."

"No, honey, we haven't gotten off the ride. You can't really stop going up and down like that and still be really alive. I mean alive now . . . not just living. This here is one item love and stunting have in common. There's no such thing as a smooth, easy road. There are bumps all along the way. You can only bypass some of them, and others you take real nice and slow. That's what Joanie and I are trying to do now. I'd bet all I've got that you and Luke can do the same."

"Go tell Luke that."

"I will, but I think you ought to tell him that yourself."

"I think you're right," she said with her first real smile of the afternoon. "But I'll give him a couple of days to cool off first."

Dodger lifted his glass and tapped it against Cat's. "Let's drink to that."

CHAPTER SIXTEEN

Dodger stepped quietly into the hospital room.

"I'm not asleep," Cat said, sitting up in bed. "Turn on the light, will you?"

Dodger flicked on the switch near the wall. He smiled across at his daughter.

"How are you feeling?" he asked, coming up to her side. He was carrying a large bouquet of roses.

"Where did you find those?" She smiled. "Peter searched all over Alonnisos the other day for them."

"Athens has more to offer than the islands."

"I wouldn't know," she said, the first note of sullenness in her voice. Dodger stuck the roses in a pitcher of drinking water and then sat down on the edge of her bed.

"You sound as grouchy as Ben did back at that hospital in San Francisco."

"Did the doctor say anything to you?" she asked

anxiously. She'd been cooped up in this room for two days. She might be sounding as grouchy as Ben, but she could also empathize with him now.

"What's your hurry, little girl? The film's over. You've got some time off."

"I wasn't planning on spending my vacation in the hospital. After fifteen years I do something dumb like this. I wouldn't mind if it had been because of a stunt," she muttered, swinging herself sideways so that she could get out of bed. "Could you hand me my crutches?"

"I thought the doctor wanted you to stay off your leg for a few more days before you started dancing around on those sticks."

"He gave me permission to visit my luxurious private bath while I'm holidaying here." She stepped down on her good right foot and carefully maneuvered her leg, done up in a cast from ankle to thigh, off the bed. Dodger gave her the wooden crutches and she hobbled off to the bathroom.

"Your head must be feeling better," he called after her. "You're back to being ornery."

"Wait till tomorrow. You ain't seen nothing yet."

Joanie came into the room, loaded down with magazines, as Cat was making her way back from the bathroom to her bed.

"How are you?" Joanie asked pleasantly.

Dodger answered for her. "Don't ask."

Cat smirked. "I'm much better, thanks. You didn't have to bring me all those magazines. I'll be out of here before I get to read them."

"Cat, the doctor says he'd like to keep you here

a few more days," Dodger said sympathetically. "That break was pretty bad, and he wants to get some more X rays. There's a chance—a small chance now—that he might have to operate to reset the bone."

"Operate? I don't want an operation. I want to get out of here. You're all flying home tomorrow, and I intend to be on that plane. Come on, Dodger, talk to the doctor."

Joanie squeezed Cat's shoulder. "Relax. The doctor is only doing what's best. Besides, Dodger and I are going to stay around and fly back with you when you're ready to go home."

"I don't want you to have to do that."

"Why don't you get some shut-eye, Cat?" Dodger put his arm around Joanie. "I'll take Joanie to lunch, and then we'll talk some more about it in the afternoon. Meanwhile, don't worry about anything."

"Sure. Why worry?" Cat grumbled.

Dodger grinned. "You never did take to hospitals. Remember when you were seven and had to have your tonsils removed? Your screaming sure gave those tonsils a good last workout before the doc finally corralled you."

"Well, I just might start screaming again."

"Give us a chance to make our getaway first." He chuckled. "Oh . . . uh . . . by the way, you want me to get in touch with anyone?"

"No, I do not want you to call Luke, Dodger. We went over that yesterday."

"You thought differently a few days before this

happened to you," he said, nodding in the direction of her leg. "After you almost blew yourself up, you said—"

"I know what I said. I changed my mind. I decided I don't want to compromise, after all. And, I don't want you to call Luke and tell him I'm in the hospital. That's final."

"Women!" Dodger threw up his hands. "I'll never understand them."

Joanie grinned. "Come on, Dodger. Let's go eat, and I'll try to enlighten you a little."

After they left, Cat picked up one of the fashion magazines Joanie had brought and began thumbing through it. She stopped a few minutes later when she realized she could not remember a thing she'd looked at.

Joanie and Dodger sat downstairs in the hospital cafeteria eating lunch. Dodger jabbed at his food for a minute and then threw his fork down.

"I don't know what to do, Joanie. That girl is pining away up there, but she's as stubborn as they come. I know what's going on, too. It's that pride of hers. She's damned if she's going to go begging."

"That's probably part of it," Joanie said, "but I think she's really scared."

"The man is in love with her, Joan. If she'll only let go of that two-fisted need to have everything her own way . . ."

"There's more to it than that. It's not only her profession at issue, it's Luke's."

272

"He's got a great profession. Stable, secure, highly respected."

"Exactly. The very opposite of Cat's world," Joanie reminded him.

"Okay. I grant you that. But Cat is a bright, sophisticated woman who could fit into Luke's world in the blink of an eye. I bet she'd knock that stuffy community on their butts. And it would probably do them some good. Luke sure as hell got knocked on his, and he admits himself he's not the same man anymore." Dodger was stretching his point a bit, but he really did think Luke was all the better for his involvement with Cat.

"If she gave up stunting completely she would end up being the one who was doing all the compromising. I thought you had a long talk with her about the importance of mutual give and take."

"I did," Dodger admitted. "I realize, too, that she's not ready to give up stunting completely. I think that's the main reason she doesn't want me to get in touch with Luke. When we had our little heart to heart about compromise, Cat was plenty upset about her close call with death, and at that point stunting had lost a lot of its appeal."

"Funny how things work out sometimes." Joanie smiled.

"Yeah." He grinned back. "I wonder how Cat would handle things if Luke did manage to find out about her accident and showed up uninvited?"

"Something tells me you're about to switch from stunt coordinator to director," Joanie said, giving him a sly look.

273

*　　*　　*

Cat was half-asleep when Liz Fuller stopped by. She crossed the room as quietly as she could and placed her neatly wrapped gift on the sidetable.

Cat heard the sound of rustling paper and turned her head in Liz's direction. "Boy, I ought to break my leg more often. People keep coming by with all sorts of goodies," Cat said groggily.

"I thought you were asleep."

"I can't sleep in this place. It's too quiet. Besides, I don't do anything all day, so how could I be tired? How about organizing an escape party for me? I'm going stir crazy."

"I can't help you escape," Liz said, swiping a chocolate candy from the ornate box on the sidetable, "but I'll take you for a spin in your wheelchair if you like."

"Thanks, but I've had my tour of the place. Believe me, once you've seen it, the desire for a second visit is nonexistent. No, I'll just lie in bed and watch my muscles atrophy for amusement."

"Oh, Cat, stop feeling so sorry for yourself. Or is that not the real reason for your rotten mood?"

"Not you, too. What is this? The Luke Eliot fan club or something?"

"I've never even met the man. Actually, as far as I can tell, since he tried to save you from doom that day in San Francisco, you've been in almost constant misery. So, just to keep the record straight, I'm no fan of his. In fact, I'd like to give him a piece of my mind for putting you through all of this torture."

"It hasn't all been misery," Cat argued, then became annoyed at Liz's grin. She'd been set up for that one.

"He must really be something. Even in my most dramatic roles, no director ever made me go through what you're suffering."

"I'll get over it."

"Or die trying?" There was no humor in her tone this time.

Cat threw Liz a searing glance.

"Okay. Okay. Maybe that was a bit dramatic. You're a terrific stunt woman. I certainly don't want to lose you. You always make me look so good. I just don't want to see you so upset that you make a stab again at another crazy stunt."

"Accidents happen when you're not being crazy, too," Cat reminded her.

Liz laughed. "You're proof positive that accidents can happen when you're not stunting."

Cat's eyes rested on the gift-wrapped package. As she reached for it, Liz caught her hand. "Save it for when I go. It's only a book to help you while away the hours."

"I hope it isn't a romance," Cat snarled.

"Speaking of romance, guess where I'm going after I fly out of here tomorrow?" Her sparkling eyes and mischievous smile were a dead giveaway.

"I don't know where you're going, but I could make an educated guess who'll be joining you."

Liz sat at the edge of Cat's bed. "I know it's too soon to make pronouncements about Peter . . . but this could be the real thing. You know some-

275

thing? I just realized that I have never really been in love before. How will I know for sure that this is it?"

"If you feel positively awful half the time and in utter ecstasy the other half, chances are it's the real thing," Cat said, grinning.

Liz bent over and kissed Cat lightly on the cheek. "Buck up, kid. The final reel isn't finished. You've still got a little footage left. Use it wisely."

Cat smiled. "I'll give it some careful thought."

"Well, I'd better be off. Peter's getting our tickets arranged. We're stopping off in Paris for a few days. *C'est romantique, n'est-ce pas?*"

"*Très romantique*," Cat said with a soft sigh.

Liz started for the door.

"Hey," Cat called to her. "Aren't you going to give me your autograph before you leave?" She stuck her cast out of the cover and laughed.

Liz came back and took the felt-tip pen off the table. With a small smile on her lips, she wrote, "To my blood sister, Stubbornness and fifty drachmas will buy you a cup of coffee in this town, but it sure as hell won't buy you love! Liz."

"That's it for my words of wisdom, sweetie. Maybe you'll pick up some more thoughts from that book I bought you." Liz gave her a sly grin.

After the star swept out of the room, Cat picked up the gift-wrapped package and undid it. When she read the title of the book, a broad smile broke out on her face.

*   *   *

276

Luke had spent the morning running around the island picking up some last-minute gifts—a lovely shawl for Teri, who was probably still angry at him for canceling out on their last date to that seminar on alcoholism, and an amusing book on the history of belly dancing he thought Max Hart would enjoy.

He was leaving in two more days. This visit to Greece had turned out to be nothing like he had ever dreamed. His weeks here had been filled with pure romance . . . and pure hell.

When he walked out on Cat that last time, he was sure that was it. How many times could someone say good-bye? He and Cat must be close to having set the record.

Oh, he had meant it each time. But this was truly the limit. Cat's brush with death had been the final, ultimate straw in a large collection of straws he'd been accumulating since their first memorable encounter. He had been furious at her for wanting to step right back in the thick of it all over again.

That was four days ago. Actually, his rage managed to take him through yesterday. That was when his anger began to give way to other feelings. It was about time, he decided, to apply to himself some of the counseling skills he'd employed with others to such good effect over the years.

When he arrived back at his bungalow in the afternoon, he was still sorting through exactly what course of action to take. On the chipped porcelain kitchen table he found a nearly indecipherable note from his cleanng lady. With the help of a neighbor he finally was able to make out that Cat was in the hospital in Athens.

His first reaction was fear. He called the hospital to find out her condition, but he did not ask to be connected to her room. He needed some time to think. When he hung up, his anger started to mount. She'd been so anxious to get right back into the thick of things that she didn't even take the time to get herself together after that close call on Skiros. Cat Roy, the woman who leaps buildings, doesn't give in to fear. Damn, she wouldn't even admit to its existence! He wouldn't be surprised if she was lying in that hospital trying to think up some great stunts she could do with a cast on her leg.

She was impossible. She was also the woman he was madly, passionately in love with. Whatever stunts she pulled, even this latest one that broke her leg, couldn't alter his feelings for her. Nor did all the good-byes they had shared. How often do fantasies come true in real life, anyway?

When Cat looked up from what she had been reading and saw Luke at her door, the first thing she did was shove the book under the covers.

"That must be quite a story," Luke said, grinning as he crossed the room.

"How did you know I was here?" she countered.

Luke didn't answer her question, but Cat had a pretty good idea who had told him.

He lifted the bottom corner of the blanket to

check her leg. His eyes flashed on Liz's writing. "Your blood sister is a smart lady."

Cat jerked her leg further under the covers. "Why did you come here?"

"I heard you broke your leg and were laid up in the hospital."

"Did you hear all the details?"

"No. I don't really want to know them."

"Of course. How could I forget?"

"Cat . . . I once told you no other woman provoked jealousy in me the way you do. Well, there's never been another person on this earth who has made me feel as angry . . . as foolish . . . as frightened as you are capable of making me feel. Sometimes I want to grab you and shake you so that you will stop making me go through all this."

He reached over and touched her cheek. "You also make me feel incredibly wonderful, and that's one feeling I never want to stop experiencing. Without you, that feeling vanishes."

"So what do we do?" she asked softly, catching hold of his hand, drawing him closer to her.

"It isn't easy to watch the woman you love jump out of buildings. Maybe I'll have to learn how to do it myself. Maybe I've been too damn conservative, too afraid to take risks all my life."

"Luke, what are you talking about?"

"If you can't beat 'em, join 'em. Isn't that how the saying goes?"

"Stop teasing."

"I mean hypothetically. Would you be able to

cope with it? Would you feel that sick, sinking feeling in your stomach every time I leaped?"

"No. If you are talking hypothetical, then no, I wouldn't panic. I would trust you. If you believed you could do it, I would. Luke, what the hell are you doing?"

He strode over to the window and opened it wide. Looking back over his shoulder at Cat, he said, "If I told you, right this minute, that I could stand on this ledge out here and jump off . . . would you be scared?"

"Luke, we're on the second floor. You fall off that ledge and you'll wind up in the bed beside me."

"How about if I tell you it's only a stunt? I've worked on it . . . perfected it . . . know it cold. Come on. Would you trust me? Could you watch me sail through space without feeling terrified?"

Her back was to the wall, and they both knew it. He would never go through with it, she told herself. He just wanted to see if she could handle it any better than he did.

"Yes. I could watch you without panicking."

"Good." He blithely swung first one leg then the other onto the ledge.

Cat could feel her heart start to pound, but she was sure he'd stop any moment.

Now he was standing up, out on the ledge. Cat's nervousness made her cry out, "Luke, you aren't a stunt man. Even if you're joking, you could accidentally fall. Luke, get inside."

"Remember when I begged you to come inside that first day? I owe you one."

Then he jumped. Cat screamed. Frantically, she extracted herself from the covers and hobbled to the window.

There was a look of pure terror on her face. It was replaced by one of shock as Luke poked his head up over the windowsill to peer at her. When she got to the window, she looked down to see that Luke was standing on a scaffolding left by the window washers. His leap had been a two-foot drop at the most.

"You . . . you . . ."

"Now remember, Cat. You said you wouldn't panic. And I did owe you that one for what you've put me through. At least this experience will be a little humbling for you. Make you more understanding of what I will have to go through every time you leave our happy home and hearth to go hurling your gorgeous body out of burning cars, off runaway horses . . . or whatever other crazy stunts you pull. A body, I might add, that I hope will bear our children one of these days."

He climbed back inside as Cat continued to glare at him. "Are you mad at me?" he whispered, coming close to her. "It was only a joke."

"At least when I pulled my stunts on you, I was truly contrite," she muttered, her anger fading as he put his arms around her. She looked him straight in the eye. "Did you mean what you said about 'home and hearth'?"

"Every word."

"It isn't going to be an easy life for either one of us. I don't know if I can handle being a psychiatrist's wife any better than you can handle being a stunter's husband."

"I don't know. There was this rush of excitement when I took that leap," he teased.

"Luke, you're crazy." She laughed, putting her arms around his neck. "You're right about one thing. I will be a lot more understanding of what you go through watching me."

"Good. See, we're making progress already." He bent and kissed her lightly. Then he drew her tightly to him for a deeper kiss.

"I don't know anything about your work. You said yourself, I wouldn't understand half the things you read and discuss. Teri Caulfield will probably stand up and denounce me at your next medical conference," she said with a small smile.

"If I can learn the inner workings of 'gags' then you can learn the works of Sigmund Freud." He lifted her in his arms and carried her back to bed.

When he pulled down the covers for her, he spotted the book she had hidden from him.

"My blood sister thought I might find it helpful reading." Cat looked at him with a broad grin.

He read the title aloud. "*The Making of a Psychiatrist.*"

Cat took the book from his hands. "I'd rather learn from a master," she whispered as she put her head on his shoulder.

He encircled her in his arms and held her tightly against him.

"Oh, Luke, it hurt so much when you walked away that day. I thought I'd never see you again."

"No more good-byes. We're responsible for this crazy script, and I think it deserves a wildly improbable ending," he said as he kissed the soft curve of her neck.

"I might give up runaway horses when I'm bearing those children," she murmured in his ear. "Who knows, one of these days I might even slow down—take over Dodger's job and just coordinate those wild stunts instead of doing them myself."

He held her at arm's length and stared into her midnight-blue eyes. "Don't get too tame. I love that spirit of yours. One of these days I might even get used to it."

"I love you," she said softly, adding with a smile, "I'm afraid right now you'll have to settle for tame. This cast is going to keep me off ledges for a while. You never did hear how it happened."

"Cat, I don't . . . okay. I guess this is lesson number one in getting my feet wet," he relented. "What stunt were you doing this time?"

"Well, there was this gag, kind of an aerial acrobatic maneuver from a helicopter. . . ." She watched his frown begin to deepen, despite his efforts to remain calm. A teasing smile played upon her lips. "I was on my way to the runway when this guy on a motorcycle shot out of nowhere and ran me down."

He broke out in laughter.

"It isn't that funny. Twenty years of doing stunts,

and my first broken bone is the result of forgetting to look both ways before I cross the street."

Hugging her to him, he said, "I guess you just can't be too careful these days."

☐ **45 SILENT PARTNER,** Nell Kincaid 17856-8-26

☐ **46 BEHIND EVERY GOOD WOMAN,** Betty Henrichs 10422-X-18

☐ **47 PILGRIM SOUL,** Hayton Monteith 16924-0-18

☐ **48 RUN FOR THE ROSES,** Eileen Bryan 17517-8-19

☐ **49 COLOR LOVE BLUE,** Diana Blayne 11341-5-22

☐ **50 ON ANY TERMS,** Shirley Hart 16604-7-15

☐ **51 HORIZON'S GIFT,** Betty Jackson 13704-7-11

☐ **52 ONLY THE BEST,** Lori Copeland 16615-2-20

$2.50 each

Candlelight

Ecstasy Romances™

- ☐ **274 WITH ALL MY HEART,** Emma Merritt 19543-8-13
- ☐ **275 JUST CALL MY NAME,** Dorothy Ann Bernard 14410-8-14
- ☐ **276 THE PERFECT AFFAIR,** Lynn Patrick 16904-6-20
- ☐ **277 ONE IN A MILLION,** Joan Grove 16664-0-12
- ☐ **278 HAPPILY EVER AFTER,** Barbara Andrews 13439-0-47
- ☐ **279 SINNER AND SAINT,** Prudence Martin 18140-2-20
- ☐ **280 RIVER RAPTURE,** Patricia Markham 17453-8-15
- ☐ **281 MATCH MADE IN HEAVEN,** Malissa Carroll 15573-8-22
- ☐ **282 TO REMEMBER LOVE,** Jo Calloway 18711-7-29
- ☐ **283 EVER A SONG,** Karen Whittenburg 12389-5-15
- ☐ **284 CASANOVA'S MASTER,** Anne Silverlock 11066-1-58
- ☐ **285 PASSIONATE ULTIMATUM,** Emma Merritt 16921-6-11
- ☐ **286 A PRIZE CATCH,** Anna Hudson 17117-2-13
- ☐ **287 LOVE NOT THE ENEMY,** Sara Jennings 15070-1-46
- ☐ **288 SUMMER FLING,** Natalie Stone 18350-2-41
- ☐ **289 AMBER PERSUASION,** Linda Vail 10192-1-16

$1.95 each

 At your local bookstore or use this handy coupon for ordering:

DELL READERS SERVICE—Dept. B469C
P.O. BOX 1000, PINE BROOK, N.J. 07058

Please send me the above title(s). I am enclosing $_____ (please add 75¢ per copy to cover postage and handling.) Send check or money order—no cash or CODs. Please allow 3-4 weeks for shipment.

Ms./Mrs./Mr._____

Address_____

City/State_____ Zip_____

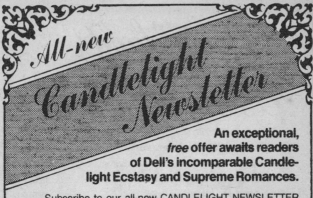